THE CINNABAR BOX

Ilil Arbel

"The Cinnabar Box," by Ilil Arbel. ISBN 1-58939-469-0, 1-58939-470-4 (electronic).

Published 2003 by Virtualbookworm.com Publishing Inc., P.O. Box 9949, College Station, TX, 77842, US.

Manufactured in the United States of America.

To Alan, with thanks. This book could have never been written without our many discussions and conversations regarding the Forest.

———————

This is an adventure story, but ecology, botany, and zoology are strong elements in its concept. It is particularly important since Wicca consider themselves Guardians of the Earth. All beasts and plants, mythological or real, are, to the best of my knowledge, researched and correct. The same applies to wizards and historical characters.

Chapter One

Crash! A shower of little boxes, bits of jewelry and other small antiques fell on Donna's head like glittering rain.

"I'm so sorry," she whispered, tears in her eyes. "I wanted to reach the shelf, and my glasses slipped and I tried to catch them – I just can't do anything right!"

Donna's mother came from the other side of the antique shop. She looked at Donna with resigned disapproval.

"Nonsense, the place is a dusty mess anyway," said old Mr. Rose, the owner. "Here, Donna, take this little box for your collection. It can't be opened, but it's pretty, isn't it?"

The box shone like a rough, dark ruby under the store's dim light, its red surface deeply carved with tiny animal figures. It must be ancient, thought Donna, speechless with admiration. Some of the carvings are a little worn and glossy, she thought. Many hands had rubbed it through the centuries . . . how mysterious . . . a treasure inside, quite possibly . . .

"Really, Mr. Rose, you shouldn't reward her for being clumsy," said Mom. "The box must be quite expensive."

"I can't sell it if it doesn't open, can I? I have had it for a long time, and these animals are beginning to annoy me! Anyway, Mrs. Williams, leave the child alone, it was just an accident," said the old man, winking at Donna.

"There may be something expensive inside, though," said Donna reluctantly.

"Finder's keeper's," said the old man. "Whatever's inside is yours, too. The box is made of Cinnabar. It's an ancient art they still use in China, layering the substance on a base, and then carving it."

"Thanks, Mr. Rose! It's so beautiful. I'll try not to break anything next time Mom brings me here," said Donna.

"I think you're getting too old to tag along when I visit shops for my clients," said Mom icily as they went to the car. "I hope you'll learn to behave more maturely at summer camp."

Donna sighed. The awful summer camp again. These dreadful girls, slim and pretty and almost grown up, same as those in the obnoxious private school she attended all year. As she entered the car she secretly wiped a tear. However, nothing escaped Mom.

"I'll never understand why you can't appreciate the advantages you are getting," said Mom. "What I wouldn't have given for this camp when I was your age . . ."

"But you were pretty and could play sports, and –"

"You could be pretty if you exercised and took

care of your hair," interrupted Mom, "and the junk food you love doesn't help either your figure or your complexion. Anyway, I have no choice. I'm attending the Italian Design Show and Dad is staying the summer in Europe as usual. What do you expect me to do with you?"

Donna wiped her eyes fiercely. "Maybe I can stay with Grandma in Florida?"

"Grandma is not up to looking after kids anymore and you know it."

"I wish Aunt Yolanda were back," said Donna sadly. "Oh, how I wish she were back. I'm sure she would have wanted me."

Mom turned and looked at her. Her enormous blue eyes flashed with fury.

"Aunt Yolanda can't break a zoological expedition to the Rain Forest in South America just to take care of a thirteen-year old who should know better," she said slowly and quietly.

"I know. But if she were here she would have wanted me to stay with her. We have such a good time when I do, really."

Mom didn't answer. The silence almost crushed Donna. She clutched the cinnabar box in a sweaty hand and gazed at the manicured lawns and well-groomed trees in the huge gardens surrounding the big houses, all planted with exactly the same flowers.

At home she went upstairs to her room and put the little box gently on the night stand, dusting it first with a tissue. The tiny carvings of camels, donkeys, lizards and other unusual animals inhabited a little world full of magical beasts, and it didn't matter one bit that it couldn't be opened.

Perhaps it would open if a prince touched it after a beautiful princess released him from enchantment, and inside they will find their wedding bands, hidden there for at least two thousand years by an evil wizard from another planet . . ."Stop!" Donna said firmly to herself. "These stupid dreams are exactly what gets you in trouble all the time. Princesses and wizards! Grow up!"

She turned on the T.V., kicked off her sneakers, and sat on the bed for a long time, clicking channels and staring at the screen without paying attention. Suddenly the doorbell rang, shattering the silence. Quick footsteps, a cheerful, familiar voice, and for a moment Donna simply did not believe her ears. It just couldn't be!

She jumped off the bed, stumbled on one of the sneakers, fell down, dropped her glasses, fumbled to pick them up, ran downstairs two steps at a time and burst into the living room, straight into the arms of Aunt Yolanda.

"How come you're here, my dear?" Mom was just saying. "We thought you planned to stay at least another month in South America."

"We finished early. I came home last week and guess what I did! No, you'd never guess. I purchased a house in the country! No more city life for me. I intend to do absolutely nothing until next fall, so naturally I came to invite Donna to stay the summer. She must help me decorate the house. It's enormous!"

Mom was quiet, almost motionless. Donna suddenly felt cold all over, her palms moist and her heart beating wildly. Aunt Yolanda smiled pleasantly. Could it be that she didn't know how much Mom detested her? Why did Mom hate her, anyway? Aunt Yolanda was Dad's sister, after all!

"That's sweet of you, Yolanda, but I've already registered and paid for her summer camp. It starts next week. I don't know . . ."

"Oh, they'll refund, darling. They always have a long waiting list for these fancy camps," said Aunt Yolanda. "And just think of the advantages! Donna will meet the children of such influential families at my new place! You have no idea who are the members of the country club, and most of Donna's age group go there instead of summer camps. These people just don't *use* summer camps. Very good for her, socially, I think. Why don't you run to your room, Donna, while I try to persuade your mom? You probably have to start thinking about the clothes you'll take no matter where you go. If you come with me you'll need some *really* elegant clothes."

"I got her a perfect wardrobe for the camp," started Mom with some enthusiasm. Donna left the room.

Donna grabbed all her clothes from the closet and threw them feverishly on the bed. She had no idea what to pack, and the suitcase Mom gave her was awfully large. She sat on the bed and stared at the mess. The new clothes were ugly and she hated them all, but looking in the mirror she decided that no clothes could make her pretty, anyway. Why didn't she look like her tall, blond mother? She tried to comb her short, fuzzy red hair to make it smooth, like Mom's, without much success. Sometimes Mom looked as if she were made of glass, beautiful, almost glowing, but brittle. Donna wouldn't have minded looking like her aunt, either. Aunt Yolanda had a lovely face, lots of wavy auburn hair, and a great figure, though she wasn't as thin as Mom. But then, Aunt Yolanda ate real food, and cakes and sandwiches, while Mom ate only salads and fruit.

A soft knock on the door, and Aunt Yolanda walked in, her emerald green eyes shining with victory. "Let's pack your bags and leave before Mom changes her mind," she said, laughing. "And take all the elegant clothes, even though we both know you'll never wear them. I don't want to hurt Mom's feelings, she took so much trouble with your wardrobe, so we'll buy you some real clothes when we get home." Donna jumped and hugged Aunt Yolanda with all her might. She wasn't going to camp!

———

Aunt Yolanda's old van glided smoothly over the country road. Donna was quiet, but the silence, this time, was friendly. The relief drained her of all emotion.

"You've no idea," she finally said. "This vile camp. I was scared to go."

"Don't be mad at Mom," said Aunt Yolanda seriously. "Her business is demanding, she has worked hard to build it from scratch, and the Italian shows are incredibly important. And you may hate fancy camps and schools, but Mom thinks it's good for you to mingle with the right crowd."

"Yes, she wants me to have what she calls

'advantages' and she buys me stuff and takes me to all these concerts and shows. But I think she's bored with me. I'm not pretty, and I don't like all these social things and I can't stand the daughters of her snooty friends."

"Well, some day you'll be very beautiful, Donna, not just pretty. You'll see. And I don't think Mom is bored with you, either, it's just that the two of you don't feel the same way about various things. You nevertheless love each other very much, and it will be better when you are older. Anyway, let's forgive Mom for wishing to give you a good future, and think about other things. I came to get you not only because I love spending the summer with you, but because the time has come to start your training in the family business."

"What family business? Dad is a diplomat, Mom is an interior designer, and you're a zoologist! There is no family business!"

"Yes there is," said Aunt Yolanda calmly. "We're Witches."

Donna laughed. "With broomsticks and pointed hats and long noses? And maybe some bubbling pots?"

"What a Medieval picture you paint," said Aunt Yolanda disgustedly. "Witches are servants of the Earth, not hags on brooms!"

Donna looked at her with amazement. It must be a joke, of course, the way they always made up stories together, but Aunt Yolanda seemed oddly serious.

"How do I know when you need me?" asked Aunt Yolanda. "You must have noticed that I always come when you are in trouble." She pulled the car to the side of the road and parked. From inside her shirt she took a heavy silver locket, and opened its little hinge. Inside was a translucent pink gemstone.

"Now, think hard, Donna. Say to yourself: I wish Aunt Yolanda were here. I really wish she were here. I'm in trouble."

Donna tried. She ran the thought through here mind two or three times. Suddenly the stone darkened, turning garnet red with fiery flashes. Donna jumped back, losing her thought. The stone slowly returned to the original pink.

"This is how I know," said Aunt Yolanda gently. "Whenever you are unhappy, the stone turns red, and becomes a little warmer."

"Does Mom know?" whispered Donna, clutching her hands together to stop their shaking.

"No. The Witchcraft trait runs in Dad's side of the family, though he did not inherit it, and doesn't even know about it. I was informed when the time came for me, and then trained by my Great Aunt Matilda. What a truly magnificent Witch she was . . . I wish you could have met her. Anyway, unless someone suspects you have inherited the Wicca talent, you are not told. This is what we call ourselves, incidentally. The true, old name is Wicca, not Witchcraft."

"Does it mean I'm a Witch?"

"You have the potential, otherwise the stone couldn't react to your thoughts. But years of training are necessary, and you succeed only if you truly wish to devote your life to this work."

"I wanted to be a rock star," said Donna, "but

this is better. Would I be able to turn people into frogs?"

Aunt Yolanda laughed as she returned to the road. "Most likely you'll protect and defend real frogs . . . look, you can see the house from here!"

Donna saw an old house, with roofs and garrets and terraces jutting out like afterthoughts. Enormous, ancient conifers touched their foliage above the roof, protecting the house like a green blanket. Aunt Yolanda parked the van in the dilapidated driveway, and as Donna jumped out she smelled the wild roses, honeysuckles and pines. The soft rustling of leaves and the bird songs were the only audible sounds.

"This is great . . . when you mentioned the country club to Mom I thought you bought a house in the suburbs. Is there really a country club? Do I have to go there?"

"The country club definitely exists, and I became a member in case your Mom wants to call us there. You know I never really lie. But it's an hour drive from here, and no, you don't have to go. We have so much work to do, decorating the house!"

"The house is splendid just the way it is," said Donna. "I must explore."

"Go ahead. I'll make a snack in the meantime. Just watch out for the rickety stairs."

She explored room after room, some filled with dusty and comfortable old furniture, some completely empty. Every window opened into the fragrant canopy of trees and vines, and cool, green light poured in. Climbing to the second floor on the half-broken stairs, Donna entered a small, bright and cheerful room that she knew immediately must be her own.

Two opened windows allowed the heavy pine branches to grow inside and press against the walls, making the room look like a tree house. On one of the branches hung a tiny antique lantern with a candle stuck in it. A white bedspread and a comfortable pile of pillows covered the bed. Two chairs, a chest of drawers, a mirror and an empty bookcase, all made of natural wood, completed the furniture. The green afternoon light moved with the branches of the trees, creating little patches and pools, constantly dancing, rolling and changing.

"Donna, come have your snack!"

Almost reluctantly, she went downstairs, and Aunt Yolanda asked "did you like your room?"

"It's awesome," said Donna. "I just love it. But how did you know that I really could come? You prepared the room for me specially, I can tell!"

"Ah, well, let's say I had a hunch. And even if you couldn't make it this time, I had plans for the future. There are some wonderful schools here, you know. How would you like to live with me until you finish high school?"

Donna was speechless. Her mouth opened and her jaw hung without any dignity or style.

"Your parents will let you stay here if I worked regularly from the house. I have three books lined up with my publisher, and the Museum people don't care if I send them their monthly publications by e- mail. Let's face facts, darling. Your Dad lives almost permanently in Europe. Your Mom is dreadfully busy. I think they feel bad about how little time they can spend with you, but these are their lives, and they really can't change now. I, on the other hand, have all the time in the world, and my favorite activity is raising you . . . and I'm family, after all, and they trust me, even if they don't always approve of me. If I told them you could go to school with the children of the 'best families' of the State, and have me take care of you, why not?"

Donna started crying. Aunt Yolanda hugged her.

"Do you really want me? You won't be able to travel to the Rain Forest if I stay with you," whimpered Donna, wiping her eyes.

"Haven't you guessed yet? I never go to the Rain Forest. At least not the one in South America. This trip I went about my Witch business to a different forest altogether. Next time I take a trip you can come along, if you agree to stay with me."

"Agree? I have never wanted anything more in my life!" Donna sobbed just a little more. Then she ate plenty of chocolate cake and ice cream, and Aunt Yolanda did exactly the same.

"Let's go upstairs and put books in your bookcase," suggested Aunt Yolanda when they finished eating. "I didn't have time to arrange them, and they're still in my room."

From under her bed, Aunt Yolanda pulled a huge cardboard box full of books. They started carrying them to Donna's room and arranging them in the bookcase. Some were old favorites, some school books, and some were mysterious, heavy books with strange titles. "Witchcraft books, of course," explained Aunt Yolanda. "We will start soon. You'll love it, it's such fun."

"The idea scares me a little," confessed

Donna. "I drop things, I break stuff. What if I have to look after bubbling cauldrons?"

"Witches don't use bubbling cauldrons. I'm rather fond of microwave ovens. Like most people, you have a wrong idea of Witches, probably because of all those ridiculous Medieval legends, not to mention the horrible Witch Trials of Salem. We are custodians of the Earth, caretakers, friends of animals and plants. We save and protect them. Of course we're born with the talent, but my Ph.D. in zoology is real, and I use this part of my education every day in my work, just as much as I use my Witch Training. I am the keeper of a very special zoo."

"A zoo! Can I go there? You know how I love zoos!" cried Donna, her eyes glowing with anticipation.

"Of course I know. I introduced you to them when you were a mere baby. Your real talent, though, I think, is with plants. Did you bring your herbarium, by the way?"

"Sure. My plant guidebooks, too. Here they are, in my backpack. I figured you have tons of interesting plants I can collect."

They brought Donna's suitcase from downstairs and began arranging her clothes. Donna unrolled the soft sweater in which she wrapped her new cinnabar box, and was about to put it on the chest of drawers, when Aunt Yolanda caught sight of it.

"My goodness, child, where did you get this?"

"I got it this morning at the antique shop where Mom goes for her clients. The owner, Mr.

Rose, gave it to me after I upset everything on one of his shelves."

"I know Mr. Rose," said Aunt Yolanda, smiling mysteriously. "In fact, I recommended him to your Mom, years ago. So he gave you this Cinnabar box . . . Did he tell you how long he had it?"

"He said he had it for years and couldn't sell it because it would not open."

"It's beautiful. Maybe some day we can figure a way to open it, who knows," said Aunt Yolanda.

"I don't mind even if it stays shut," said Donna, looking affectionately at the little carved animals.

They took a walk in the woods and identified about ten species of plants and flowers with the guidebook. Donna could always remember an amazing number of Latin names. The woods were wild and untouched, a naturalist's heaven. When the sun set they went in for dinner, and cooked in the rather unsophisticated kitchen.

"What we need is more modern equipment," said Aunt Yolanda. "Let's go to town tomorrow and shop. Now, where shall we eat?"

Deciding to eat on the veranda, Donna brought the little old lantern with the candle from her room. Huge white Luna Moths fluttered around them, and they could see a few bats on their way to some hidden water body. They heard the unmistakable sounds of flying squirrels, too.

"It will be so beautiful in winter, when the snow covers the pines, and the wind blows in the tree-tops. We'll have pine wood fires in the fireplace, and the house will smell like a forest," said Aunt

Yolanda.

"I want to stay so much," said Donna wistfully. "Even if I have to study both regular school and Witchcraft and do double homework it will be so much fun. Do you really believe they'll let me stay?"

"I have no doubt of it. I've never failed to persuade them to do anything I want," said Aunt Yolanda. She went into the house and came back with a package.

"I have something you will need," said Aunt Yolanda and took a heavy silver locket, very much like her own, from the package.

"There is no stone in it yet, because you must either find or win it yourself. But you should start wearing the locket regularly."

The old silver glowed with a dark shine. Strange carvings of flowers and tendrils wrapped all around it, and the flowing shape of a ribbon, or a river, ran through the foliage. Donna put it reverently around her neck and it felt just right, as if she had been wearing it for years.

"I'll never take it off," she whispered with awe, rubbing the old carving gently. "Thank you so much . . . I feel like a Witch already when I wear it."

"I thought you would, darling. You have it in you, trust me. It just has to be developed, like any other talent."

———

Moonlight filled Donna's room with rivers of milk and liquid silver. She hung the tiny lantern back on the pine branch that entered the room, and the touch released the powerful, resinous scent of the pine needles. Unwilling to disturb the magic by turning on the light, she undressed in the semi-darkness, relaxed on the soft white pillows, and breathed the cool night air deeply. Two fireflies found their way into the pine branch and twinkled like little distant stars right inside the room. I don't want to fall asleep, Donna thought, looking at the two blinking, golden dots. I'll miss something wonderful . . . I want to stay up all night . . . She drifted off on a dark wave of dreamless sleep.

———————

The heavy wooden door burst open, and the prime minister ran into the queen's room with such unseemly haste that he tripped over his long robe and fell down. Fortunately he was plump and bouncy and so was not really hurt. Paying no attention to his undignified position, he cried: "They found the Cinnabar Box! Camellia and Bartholomew – they just called!"

The queen looked affectionately at her old friend, a momentary smile lifting the patient sadness from her huge black eyes. She poured a glass of water from an earthenware jar and handed it silently to the prime minister. The queen was tall, thin, and not very young. She wore a simple white robe and had no crown on her graying black hair. But no one could mistake her for anyone but a great queen, daughter of an ancient dynasty.

The queen removed a black cloth from a crystal ball, mounted on a golden box with black buttons. She walked slowly to the window and looked out at the desert. Outside, the hot wind blew vigorously, driving the dust against the heavy glass of the window pane. The queen gazed at the gray and stormy sky, covered with clouds that never rained, and waited until the crystal ball started to shimmer with swirling streams of white smoke. Suddenly the face of a camel appeared in the ball.

"Camellia, my dear," said the queen, touching and adjusting the black buttons on the crystal ball. "I am glad to see you are safe. This has been a long assignment."

"Thank you, Your Majesty," said Camellia. "I am happy to report that we have found the Cinnabar box. Mr. Rose, an owner of an antique shop, had it for years and didn't know what to do with it, though he suspected something. He gave it to a young girl, named Donna. I believe he saw us spying on him, and I think he understood, but we couldn't communicate. You know how it is in their bizarre reality."

"And will the girl give you the Cinnabar box if you explain the need?"

"It's a bit more complicated than that, Your Majesty. Let me explain . . ."

Chapter Two

The red sunset poured through the dark pines and turned the new white dishes rosy red. Donna sighed contentedly as she finished her second slice of warm cherry pie topped with vanilla ice cream, and curled into a small ball in the faded cushions of the old wicker chair.

"The new microwave did a good job on this cherry pie," said Aunt Yolanda.

"And the little town is so cute," said Donna. "The housewares store looks like a doll's house. By the way, did you notice I didn't break anything?"

"Must be the Wicca locket," said Aunt Yolanda innocently, sipping her coffee. "Pure magic."

Donna laughed, but suddenly looked apprehensively at her aunt. It could just be true, she thought.

"The Country Club looks as boring as the one Mom belongs to," she said quickly.

Aunt Yolanda laughed. "I guess that's why you suggested visiting it some other time, perhaps? You're right, anyway. We have much more important things to do. First, I want to tell you about my zoo."

She brought a large photo album from the living room, and opened it at random. Donna stared at a clear, sharp photograph of a large flightless bird. A somewhat familiar bird, but she couldn't quite place it or read the Latin name scribbled under the photograph.

Next appeared a photograph of a sea-turtle, again different from the usual. The next was a gorgeous tiger, but it had large, menacing teeth, unlike the tigers in zoos, circuses, or zoology books.

"Stop one minute," she said, intrigued. "I have seen this tiger somewhere. Wait – it was on the cover of a science fiction book called *Attack of the Sabertooth-Tiger Amazons of Tau Ceti,* I think . . . excellent book, I really liked it . . . sabertooth! Are you kidding me? They are extinct! They all died thousands of years ago! How can you have a photograph?"

"Didn't you recognize the Dodo bird? It's just as extinct as the sabertooth tiger. I am the keeper of a zoo of extinct animals. We take them from the past, transport them to one of our special zones in an alternate reality, and protect them for a safe future in certain realities where they will be ecologically appropriate."

"A couple of years ago I saw a stuffed Dodo in the American Museum of Natural History in New York City," said Donna. "But I never suspected they were saved. The museum bird made me cry, and the other kids laughed at me."

"You will enjoy meeting the flock. We have a whole bunch of them in the zoo, tame and friendly. They love to eat out of your hand and follow you

21

wherever you walk, like a row of ducklings. Actually, the zoo is more of a natural preserve. No cages. Witches disapprove of cages. Besides, the animals will eventually be set free, as I said before, so they must remain independent."

"I can't believe it," said Donna suddenly, the blood draining from her face. She felt cold all over. "It can't be real. It's a joke after all. Witches - no. No way."

"You want proof?" said Aunt Yolanda, amused. "You know it's all true. You are just terrified."

"Maybe. There must be many horrible dangers in your work," said Donna.

"Yes, there is plenty of danger and excitement in being a Witch. But danger exists in your father's line of work, too, and in many other fields. If you are a doctor, or a nurse, you can catch diseases. Pilots can crash. Police officers are always at risk. Professional hazards! I don't worry about them until I must."

"So when are we going to visit the zoo?"

"First, you must learn to move between realities. It will take about two weeks. Do you want more ice cream? I am going to get a second cup of coffee."

"Move between realities? Is it done by space traveling?"

"No. It is done by thinking in a special way. We'll start working on it tomorrow, but just for fun, watch the cherry pie." She closed her eyes, and sat motionless. The pie suddenly shimmered, then became transparent, then completely disappeared. Donna stared at the white dish, covered with nothing but crumbs and smears of cherry filling. Aunt Yolanda opened her eyes and smiled at Donna's dumbfounded expression. "This is no slight of hand. The pie is on my desk at the zoo. Let's bring it back before Gilbert, our pet lemur, eats it. He loves pie." She closed her eyes again, and the pie reappeared, first transparent, than shimmery, than solid. Donna touched it gingerly with an uncertain finger. "Look!" she said. "There are teeth marks on it!" "Nothing to worry about," said Aunt Yolanda. "Gilbert took a bite. Shall I send him a nice large piece? He is somewhat overweight, and our vet has told my assistant that we feed him too much . . . Oh, well . . . I really don't see why Gilbert should be skinny, since he's not going back to the wild." She cut a piece, put it on a napkin, and closed her eyes. The piece vanished. "We travel the same way," continued Aunt Yolanda, "by thinking, only we send ourselves – now what in the world is going on? Look up in the sky!"

The sky suddenly lost its golden sunset and a huge, heavy cloud snuffed out the light. Heavy purple lightening pulsated at its edges, and a deafening thunder rumbled throughout the woods. The cloud was so low it seemed to touch the tops of the trees. A violent gust of wind swept all the new dishes to the veranda's floor, but in the wind's fury Donna couldn't even hear them breaking. The cloud oozed heavily down the trees, covering everything with soot-colored fog. It deposited a filthy layer on the broken dishes, the blood-red filling of the crushed cherry pie, and the white puddle of melted ice cream.

"Run into the house," screamed Aunt Yolanda, barely audible above the relentless thunder. She leaned to clutch Donna's shoulder and shove her inside, but it was too late. The sooty fog surrounded and separated them. Donna tried to grab her aunt, but the fog was slippery and oily and its sticky waves moved constantly like a giant smoke ring. "Run!" screamed Aunt Yolanda again. "Hide in the cellar!" But Donna, paralyzed with terror, couldn't move. She stared helplessly at the fog and saw a giant purple face outlined just above her struggling aunt. The face grinned viciously with its toothless dark blue mouth and its hollow, yellow-green eyes winked at Donna. Then the fog lifted into the air, carrying Aunt Yolanda with it, and rose high above the trees. Donna lost consciousness and fell heavily on the veranda's floor.

Some time later, Donna finally stirred weakly. She couldn't move yet, but had partially regained consciousness and vaguely heard a conversation that obviously started a while ago.

" . . . but she is too young. Think of the danger . . ."

"She has to be young, you silly old camel. You know that perfectly well."

"I am not a silly old camel. I am only four thousand, three hundred and eighty two years old, and it is not even middle-age for one of my species."

"Four thousand, three hundred and eighty *five*. We are the same age, remember? Who are you kidding?"

"All right, already! But we have to wake the girl up."

"I am awake, I think," said Donna groggily.

Next to her crouched two large animals. A well-groomed camel, wearing a flower behind her ear and a pearl necklace, and a disheveled gray donkey in a dirty straw hat.

"I am sorry if we startled you, but we had to see you. You are the first owner of the Cinnabar box who happens to be a child. We cannot talk to adults in this weird reality," said the camel.

"Sometimes neither can I," said Donna sleepily. "Except for Aunt –" she suddenly woke up completely – "Aunt Yolanda! She was kidnaped! A black cloud got her . . ."

"We know," said the camel sympathetically. "It's all connected to the Cinnabar box. We will do everything we can to save your aunt . . ."

"More important than any aunt is returning the Cinnabar box to the rightful owner," growled the donkey. "Unfortunately, we are not allowed to simply steal it."

"Bartholomew!" said the camel in an injured tone. "We are not thieves!"

"Yes, yes," said the donkey rudely. "I have heard all this nonsense before. Neither the queen nor the prime minister know how to get things done. Rules and regulations . . ."

"What's in the box?" interrupted Donna.

"A key. The box can only be opened under certain conditions . . . But I can't tell you more now. The question is, do you agree to return it to the real owner?" said the camel.

"Of course. But how do we get there?"

"We? You don't have to go. You only have to take us to the edge of your reality. We need you to translate in case we have to talk to an adult . . ." said the camel

"If you want the box, Ms. ah, Camel, you take me with you. I am not deserting Aunt Yolanda."

"You see?" said the camel anxiously. "She will be in serious danger."

"Who cares?" said the donkey. "If she is killed, she is killed, I say—as long as the queen gets the key. And anyway, the girl is a Wicca, right? These Wicca take chances all the time. Part of their job."

For a moment Donna was taken aback. "I am not yet trained in Wicca, or in switching realities," she admitted.

"You will ride on my back," said the camel resignedly. "I will fly you there. There is no other way to cross the desert. And we can get you through the Reality Barrier, too." The camel slowly spread a pair of magnificent wings, the color of pearls. Each feather shone like a delicate rainbow.

"How beautiful you are," said Donna admiringly.

The donkey laughed. "Do you really think so, Wicca? This old camel will be your friend forever!"

The camel looked at him disdainfully. "Be quiet. We should introduce ourselves properly. My name is Camellia Baat-Laila, and this rude donkey is Bartholomew Ben-Harun. Don't pay attention to his stupid jokes, please, they are quite out of place under the circumstances, but he is not so bad when you get to know him. We have been brought up together, believe it or not, and trained together as agents of our queen."

"I just look so much younger, don't I?" said

Bartholomew and winked at Donna. Camellia glared at him without word and adjusted her pearls daintily.

"Let me get a few things for the trip," said Donna. She hastily threw some clothes into her backpack, and put on an old denim jacket that had a few buttoned pockets. In the pockets she stuck the Cinnabar box and a spare pair of glasses.

"Take a hat," advised Bartholomew. "Only tough old camels can manage without hats in the desert. Even I need one. The sun will destroy someone like you." She searched feverishly, and finally found an old gardening hat, a dilapidated straw affair with a torn silk rose. Bartholomew laughed at the sight and said that it was better than nothing, but she did look stupid in it. Donna ignored him, climbed on Camellia's furry back and wrapped her arms around the camel's neck. The animals spread their wings and rose into the air together.

This was no airplane ride. They flew crazily through the tree branches which lashed at Donna's face, over the dirt road and into the dark blue night. Camellia swayed and dipped as she flew, the way normal camels do when they walk. Donna shut her eyes and tightened her grip as Camellia swerved around an electric line. They rose higher, the trees and lights became smaller, and the earth slanted and dropped back. The moon and the stars, gigantic, luminous and undisturbed by city lights, washed the trio with a river of white light as they flew with immense speed.

Hours later, the moon was at their back and Donna's numb body sensed that they were descending. They flew no longer above the trees, but between their heavy trunks, painted white on one side. Dark shadows striped the forest's floor like the pelt of a white tiger. The trees spread out, and the animals floated to the steep edge of a river bank, covered with white mists. Finally landing, Camellia crouched on the bank and Donna stepped down, every bone and muscle stiff and hurting.

"This is it," said Camellia. "The Reality Barrier. We must go quickly. Follow me and hold tightly to my neck." They stepped into the mist. Donna felt the dank air surround and touch her with wet, warm fingers, as if testing whether to allow her through. Head down and with heavy tread, she trudged against the resisting wall of a wet substance. Her face felt cold and clammy, with drops of the unknown liquid condensing on it, and at every step the rocky ground became more slippery. She could barely see through the fogged lenses of her glasses. Worse, her mind felt muffled, confused, as if time stopped and she had been plodding for an eon, hypnotized by the mist.

Suddenly Donna heard a cry and a heavy thud - Camellia stumbled and fell on the wet ground. "Don't panic!" grumbled Bartholomew. Supporting Camellia from one side, he directed Donna to do the same from the other. She pushed with all her might, and together they managed to raise the injured camel, and helped her hobble forward on three legs, as she leaned on them with her wings.

Through the haze of sluggishness that descended on her, something tagged at Donna's consciousness. Her hand automatically went to her

jacket pocket to touch the Cinnabar box. "Stop!" she
screamed. "I lost the box!" Crawling on all fours, she
searched the wet ground desperately. Back and
forth, she ran her hands over the slippery rock
surface of the ground, shaking and crying. Then her
glasses fell off her wet face, and she heard the soft
thud as they hit the ground just beneath her.
Picking them up, she felt the rough, carved surface
of the Cinnabar box right under her bruised hand.
She stuck it in her pocket, sobbing and trembling,
and they walked on.

At last the mist began to thin, and suddenly
vanished as if it had never existed. On the other
side of the Reality Barrier Donna saw the desert.
She had visited deserts before, and expected to see
the beautiful colors and interesting rock formations
she had encountered there, but this desert was
different. The immense, empty plain stretched into
infinity, baked to an even dusty gray, and
tormented by a constant, burning wind. Clouds of
fine sand settled on Donna's glasses. The dry air
hurt the inside of her nose and mouth. She gasped,
struggling to adjust her breathing, and turned back
to see what the Reality Barrier looked like from the
desert's side. It swirled like an ominous wall of gray
dust, made of hundreds of whirlwinds blown
together. She shuddered and averted her eyes.

"Is the whole place like this?" She asked,
coughing as she spoke.

"Well," said Bartholomew, "here and there we
have an oasis, but that's it. This is the problem, you
see. The desert is taking over the entire land. If
Camellia's leg is not broken, we will go to an oasis

right now."

"It's not broken, just bruised. I can fly," said Camellia.

"Not so fast," said a scratchy, high voice behind them. They were surrounded by a group of lizard-like beings. They had gray-green, scaly skin, much like the dark armor they were wearing. They stared at the travelers with large, dark eyes with no pupils.

"Not you again," sighed Bartholomew contemptuously. "Give it a break, reptile. Once again you are detaining us against our will and the queen will object."

"Shut up, Ben-Harun," said the soldier. "You know who wants to see you. He has every right – you and Bat-Laila are trespassing in his land with this small ugly human. But what makes you think we are holding you against your will? The Vizier is so hospitable! He just wants you to pay a social visit before you go to your precious queen. Have a nice meal."

"We don't want to see him," said Bartholomew. "You can tell your renegade Vizier that we are in a hurry and not interested in his gracious hospitality. And this land, reptile, is not his and never will be."

The soldier produced a weapon that looked like a carved ivory stick and pointed it at the donkey. Bartholomew shut up. Silently, the lizards tied Camellia's and Bartholomew's wings with a heavy rope and led them away, motioning Donna to follow. They walked for hours, and Donna, exhausted, kept stumbling and falling. Finally one of the lenses of her glasses broke. The lizards laughed.

"Is there anything we can do?" asked the prime minister. "The Vizier will kill them!"

"What can we do, my friend?" said the queen resignedly. "We have no weapons, no soldiers, not even strong magic is left in our hands. Let's continue searching the crystal ball for Senior Witch Yolanda. I am sure she has been brought here. Her power is our only hope."

"Your Majesty, zoom first on the travelers, though. I want to check how they are."

The queen obligingly adjusted the black buttons. A small picture appeared. They hovered over the ball together, and saw the lizards, sound asleep, and the two animals tied up, huddled together. One lizard stood guard at a little distance. It was obvious that the soldiers did not bother to tie Donna, probably assuming she could do nothing to save herself in the middle of the desert.

"What is the girl doing?" whispered the prime minister, puzzled.

"She is pulling something out of her pocket," said the queen. "I can't tell what it is. She is crawling toward Camellia. Wait, I'll adjust the sound."

She played with the black buttons. "Camellia," they heard Donna whisper, "I saved the broken lens from my glasses. Let me cut the ropes they tied you with."

The queen and the prime minister looked at

each other.

"True Wicca resourcefulness," said the queen. "Senior Witch Yolanda will be proud of her."

"If Senior Witch Yolanda is alive," said the prime minister sadly, as he watched Donna cutting Bartholomew's ropes.

"In my heart I feel she is alive," whispered the queen. "I truly do."

The two animals quietly stretched their sore muscles. Donna climbed silently on Bartholomew's back, and wrapped her arms around his neck. Then the animals spread their wings simultaneously and took to the air. The sentry started running toward them, screaming, and one of the other lizards woke up and grabbed Camellia's bruised leg. She dragged him with her into the air, wobbling, kicking and fighting to shake him off. However, much of her strength was lost through the injury, and the reptile managed to hang on. The queen and prime minister saw him pull a short knife from his belt, and attempt to stab Camellia's leg. At that moment, Bartholomew dived directly under Camellia, almost losing Donna, and aimed a powerful kick at the lizard with his back leg. The lizard let go, screaming as he fell to the ground, and the animals flew away into the gray distance, their image vanishing from the crystal ball.

Chapter Three

A few spindly date palms, nine black tents, and a small water hole did not fulfil Donna's expectations of a lush, romantic desert oasis. In the old videotapes she loved to rent, a respectable oasis flaunted silk curtains, gleaming jewels, lovely princesses, and transparent veils. Most important, an impossibly handsome sheik invariably made an appearance, preferably on a silvery-white or charcoal-black horse. Nevertheless, she heartily welcomed this inappropriate oasis when the animals finally landed. Her body, already unaccustomed to such rigorous exercise as the hike with the lizards, clearly indicated a strong dislike toward the second opportunity of flight on the backs of winged animals.

Instead of the expected handsome sheik, an old woman came out of a tent, carefully closing the flap again behind her, probably to protect the inside from the ever-present, blowing sand. A charming, welcoming smile illuminated her tired, deeply lined face.

"Agents Camellia and Bartholomew," she said, her voice rich and melodious, "what joy to see you again, and with a lovely young guest, too. It's an honor to meet you, Donna. Come in and rest."

"How do you know my name?" asked Donna, surprised.

"I have received the news from my cousin, the prime minister," explained the woman, handing Donna an earthenware mug full of unexpectedly cold water. "He saw you in the queen's crystal when you escaped from the Vizier's soldiers, and realized that you will come to this oasis to rest, as it is the nearest to the enemy's territory. So of course he transmitted to my crystal immediately."

Donna was too hungry and tired to even pretend to understand, so she gulped the water down, took a sweet date-cake from a reed basket and furtively looked at her surroundings. The tent had almost no furnishing. A threadbare carpet on the floor, a few pillows to sit on, jars, pots and cooking utensils on a wooden workbench, and an old leather storage trunk, were the only objects she could see. A large crystal ball stood on the trunk, with a black cloth half covering it. This doesn't make sense, Donna thought. Why should the cousin of a prime minister live in a tent and be so poor? Before she could ask any further questions, a young girl quietly entered the tent, carrying a tray laden with a big pile of flat bread, a jar of fragrant olive oil mixed with herbs, and a plate of hard white cheese.

"My granddaughter Jessamine," said the old woman to Donna. "Shall we have dinner? I apologize for offering so little, but our land is extremely poor." She handed hot, moist towels to the guests to clean their hands and hooves.

"We are grateful for the gracious hospitality," said Camellia, daintily picking a piece of bread with her freshly cleaned hoof. She dipped the bread in the oil and tasted it. No one would have guessed, observing her impeccable manners, how hungry and sore the poor camel really felt.

"What's good enough for our queen, when she visits here, is surely more than sufficient for this untrained small Wicca," said Bartholomew, winking cheerfully at Donna. She laughed. Restored freedom obviously returned Bartholomew to his usual rude style, but Donna didn't mind it anymore.

She bit into a piece of cheese, full of sharp spices that brought tears to her eyes, and quickly stuffed her mouth with flat bread to relieve it. "It's delicious" she said enthusiastically, forgetting herself and speaking with her mouth full. Jessamine laughed. "I made it from our goat's milk," she said. "I am so glad you like it."

"You can cook?"

"Certainly. I baked the flat bread, too. Most of the people are away, tending our camels and looking for fresh grazing grounds. Only grandmother and I are here to look after the camp, so she teaches me how to do everything."

"I always wanted to learn, particularly how to bake cherry pies," said Donna, impressed.

"I have never seen cherries," said Jessamine sadly, "only in books. We can grow dates, olives, and pomegranates, because they can stand the dryness. Once in a while a fig tree makes it."

"You have the same plants we do in our reality," commented Donna. "It's a very similar world. You know, it's funny, but I'm getting used to the idea of alternate realities."

"You must be tired," said grandmother kindly after the ravenous trio finished eating. "Jessamine, take Donna to your tent for the night, and I will arrange for Agents Camellia and Bartholomew."

Jessamine's tent was similar to her grandmother's, slightly smaller, and just as neat and clean. Instead of cooking supplies, the workbench supported baskets of yarn and needlework supplies and tools – a sewing basket, knitting needles, a lap loom, a spinning wheel, and crochet hooks, all arranged in perfect order. Donna leaned comfortably on a soft floor pillow, watching the girl take out blankets from a beaten leather trunk.

"Jessamine, are you very tired? Before we go to sleep, can you tell me a little about your country?" she asked.

"Of course," said the girl. She lit a small oil lamp, sat cross legged on the floor, and pulled a basket filled with yarn toward herself. "I will work as we talk, though. This blanket must be finished." She started manipulating a bone-colored, delicately carved crochet hook with incredible speed. The hovering light of the little flame illuminated the dark blue blanket magically growing under the skillful hands, and Jessamine's neatly braided black hair. "You can do so many things, Jessamine," said Donna admiringly. "How old are you?"

"Fourteen," said Jessamine. "I should be learning other things, since Grandmother is Wicca, too, but the magic has been torn from our land by the Vizier. He is so incredibly powerful, Donna. Even the queen cannot exercise her magic. She tried to work against him with all our Wicca, in organized groups, but even their combined power failed. He controls magic by sound, with a different system than we do. It is actually named Sound Magic."

"I don't know much about any system yet," confessed Donna. "What is Sound Magic?"

Jessamine sighed. "It's awful. Sound Magic is very old, some even call it primitive. Grandmother told me that in your reality, for example, Sound Magic was used by Northern wizards who practiced power over the ocean. A wizard's shriek, or wail, could produce a storm. Different sounds create different results."

"What kind of results?"

"Well, even without magic, you must have seen the trick of shattering glass by a very high-pitched scream or even a song? And you know that the tremendously loud noise produced by powerful bells can deafen, or even kill you, if you are too close to them? And surely you know that the vibrations of many people marching in unison over a bridge could destroy it? Think what can be done when the element of magic is added to such power."

"And the Vizier uses it to hurt people."

"Yes. Without Wicca controls. We hoped to gain help from Senior Witch Yolanda –"

"My aunt!" shouted Donna, jumping to her feet. "What do you know about her whereabouts?"

"Nothing. When we tried to contact her, he must have intercepted the message. Perhaps that is why she was kidnaped. We may bear the blame, Donna."

Donna sat down again. Sadly, she listened to the sound of the wind beating against the tent.

"No, Jessamine. I don't think so. Camellia said he kidnaped her because of me – I am carrying the Cinnabar box."

"That is possible, too. The Cinnabar box must contain something crucial to the return of the water, and the Vizier wants the planet to remain a desert."

"Why? Even if he wants to rule the planet, wouldn't he be better off with food, and water, and forests, and animals?"

"No. Only when the land is dry he can dig our planet for the precious minerals it contains in such quantity. And he doesn't live here all the time, you know. He takes the treasures to his real home in a different reality."

"Did he actually manage to take away the water with his power?"

"Well, we don't know, but we think so. You must understand that in this reality some people and animals live a very long life –"

"I heard Camellia and Bartholomew talk about being a few thousand years old, but I thought they were joking."

"No. It's true. Grandmother, who is really my great-great-great-something grandmother, is over three-hundred years old. She remembers how green our land used to be, though I, of course, have only known it as a desert. The water supply of our entire planet depends on a great river that periodically overflows. You have rivers like that in your own reality – I learned about them when I met Senior Witch Yolanda. Our great river connects to and feeds every other water source. If the river does not overflow, nothing can grow. At some point, after the Vizier left the queen's service, the river changed its habits. One year it didn't overflow. Another year it sank deeper into the ground. Finally, it disappeared. Other water sources followed, of course, and by now, we are near total collapse."

"What's the great river's name?" asked Donna.

"It is just called the great river – funny, I never thought of it, it's the only body of water we have that has no name," said Jessamine slowly. "Perhaps – no. It can't be. The queen would have figured it out, wouldn't she?"

"Figure what out?" said Donna curiously.

"In Wicca, much depends on naming things. To know the true name is to know the essence of a thing, to be able to manipulate it. Perhaps the Vizier can control the river because we didn't protect it. I just don't know what to think," said Jessamine.

"I see," said Donna thoughtfully. "You know a lot about magic, Jessamine."

"Well, I have been studying the Wicca books with Grandmother for over two years. We can't practice, but some day, if the magic returns, I will know the theory and then I can start working on the practical matters."

"So you can help me," said Donna with sudden determination. "If we work together, you will tell me what to do, and I will able to do it. Since I come from a different reality, contact with the Vizier has not yet drained my magic away, if I have any to begin with."

Jessamine stared at her. "What do you want to do?"

"I want to go to where the Vizier really lives. I bet he keeps Aunt Yolanda there. You can direct me, and I will leave the Cinnabar box with Camellia and Bartholomew."

"It's incredibly dangerous, Donna. The chances of coming back alive are slim."

"We can save your planet, Jessamine, not to mention Aunt Yolanda. Are you scared?"

"Yes, I am. Terribly scared. But I will go anyway, Donna. It's worth it."

"I am scared too. We are in real trouble. I wish Aunt Yolanda were here," said Donna. "How I wish she were here . . . " she smiled sadly. These words always worked when Aunt Yolanda could read her Wicca Stone. In this reality the stone may or may not reveal Donna's thoughts, even if she could be sure that Aunt Yolanda was alive. For the first time, Donna was not sure of that. What would life be like without Aunt Yolanda, her cheerful smile, her steady support, her unconditional love?

Tears came to her eyes and she could not suppress them. They flowed and a small sob attracted Jessamine's attention. She looked up from her crochet work to see Donna covering her face with her hands, her shoulders shaking. She put her work aside, went to Donna, and hugged the crying girl with silent understanding. The tent shook as the wind went on beating it and throwing sand and pebbles against the fabric.

———————

"I just can't bear it, Your Majesty," said the prime minister brokenly as he gazed at the crystal.

"This brave little girl. Look at her crying for her aunt. We have no right –"

"She chose to come, my friend," said the queen. "She may be a little girl, but she has Wicca honor. And look at your niece Jessamine comforting her. *This* little girl lost her parents in the fight to save our land. See how brave, how strong she is. Never a complaint, never a tear, hungry and exhausted half the time."

The prime minister stealthily wiped his own tears. "After Jessamine's parents were killed while trying to save the river dam, I wanted her to live in the palace, but she chose to help Grandmother."

"I know, my friend. Did you think I could forget her courage and determination? And some day we will reward them both, I hope. Please don't cry – we do what we can. But without Donna's help we will all die. Who knows, she may be able to find Senior Witch Yolanda."

"Two little girls against the Vizier and his violent Sound Magic, Your Majesty?"

"A butterfly, batting its wings in the forest, can cause a chain of events that may change the weather thousands of miles away."

"I believe you are using a parable, Your Majesty. How does it relate to the great danger awaiting these two little girls?"

"Two little girls, whispering to each other in another reality, may interfere with the sound vibrations the wizard may have set up with his loathsome shrieking wail in this reality, Prime Minister."

———————

The girls stole into Grandmother's tent, carrying the Cinnabar box and a written note of explanation wrapped around it. Grandmother and the animals were sound asleep on their blankets. Donna put the little packet on a clean plate on the workbench, and the girls crept out of the tent and returned to Jessamine's to attempt the reality shift.

"Not so fast," they heard a voice. Bartholomew was sitting on a pillow inside their tent, his straw hat pulled low on his forehead.

"Oh, no," said Donna. "How did you manage that? We woke you up, right?"

"Not exactly. I snooped when you thought you were alone in your tent, and then pretended to sleep in mine. I knew you would be up to something. I don't trust you, Wicca, and I am coming with you to see that you don't mess everything up. Camellia will take the Cinnabar box to the queen."

"It's tremendously dangerous, Agent Bartholomew," said Jessamine respectfully.

"Do you think I will let two insignificant Wicca make trouble without trying to save the day?"

"Thank you, Bartholomew," said Donna. "You are a real friend."

"Ha!" sniffed the donkey. "I just know you can't manage without me. Besides, can you imagine how it will annoy Camellia? I can't miss that!"

Jessamine opened a small wooden box and took out a heavy, cloth-bound notebook. "My grimoire," she explained. "A Wicca spell book. I copy everything I learn into it. Each of us has her own grimoire. It's much more powerful than a printed book of other people's spells, because it's personal and geared to our own style. I will take it with me."

"Should we pack anything else?" asked Donna.

"What for?" scoffed Bartholomew. "Either we accomplish everything right away, or we are dead. We won't need any equipment."

Jessamine studied a page carefully, than tucked the book into her belt's pouch. "Donna, I will tell you what to do, and you will follow exactly, repeating the words, and actions, exactly as I describe them. Agent Bartholomew, please do not utter a sound, because anything you say may alter the coordinates. Stand near me. We must stay in physical contact."

She took off a ring, mounted with a small crystal ball, and slipped it on Donna's finger. She put her arms around the donkey and the girl.

"Donna, stare at the ball. Blink as little as possible, and allow your eyes to get tired. Focus on the center of the ball."

Small lights appeared in the ball, dancing, fleeting here and there, growing and expanding.

"Donna, create a fog in your mind. Think fog, mist, grayness."

Gray fog materialized in the ball, easily, effortlessly, gracefully. It filled the ball.

"Donna, make the fog envelop us. Think coolness, mistiness, grayness around us. All three of us. It's coming out of the ball to embrace us."

The fog drifted out of the ball like a tiny tornado. It grew into a mantle of soft, swirling wind. It caressed and encircled the trio.

"Donna, create the coordinates in your mind and project them into the ball. See the numbers in the ball. 003-67-8-4. 003-67-8-4. 003-67-..."

Red, glowing numbers appeared in the ball. They shifted and moved, but were firmly planted inside the gleaming glass.

"Donna. Now. Take us there. We are following the coordinates. See us following the numbers."

They stood on a windswept beach, illuminated by the pale light of an early afternoon. Black tar and rank, limp seaweeds mixed in filthy shallow pools and on the wet sand. Blue-black water mirrored sunless sky. The sound of the wind mingled with the shrieks of sea-birds.

"Done," said Jessamine flatly. "You are good at switching realities, Donna."

Donna gazed stupidly around her, blinking and shaking. Bartholomew laughed. "Where are we?" she whispered.

"Wizards' School Island," said Jessamine. "That's the Vizier's permanent home. He studied here years ago and decided that he liked the miserable place. Wizards come here from all realities, so I guess he enjoys the company."

"It seems deserted."

"All activity takes place underground, and only at night. We will have to go to the school to get directions to the Vizier's home. I know where the school is."

They followed her into a cove lodged between rugged cliffs. A large, dark hole in the ground gaped at them. No gate, no sentry. Anyone who chose to take the risk could go down.

They descended the slippery, winding stairs. The rock walls emitted the odor of brine and seaweeds, and the air became increasingly suffocating.

Finally they reached a huge, cavernous chamber cut directly into the rock. Heavy slabs of rock, serving as desks, supported many books, quantities of paper, and various writing tools, but no computers or typewriters. Donna opened a book at random. It contained nothing but blank paper. Suddenly, letters leaped into the paper from nowhere, and the page blazed with fiery red and green words, written in an unfamiliar language. After a few minutes, the writing disappeared, and the page turned by itself. New words appeared on it, stayed for a short time, and vanished.

"More instruction appears on the walls at night," said Jessamine. "The same red and green letters. It stays there all night, and the students can copy it. Than it disappears for the day."

"No teachers?"

"Not visible ones, anyway. Here, I have found the book of locations and coordinates," said Jessamine. "As it includes jails and current lists of prisoners, perhaps it will tell of Senior Witch Yolanda."

"Can you read the language?"

"Yes. Here is the address of the Vizier's home. We have to follow the path by the cove to the low hill in the west. Coordinates 52-1-6. Write it down, just in case, but I don't think we should use the crystal ball here, we might be intercepted. We'll have to walk, or fly. Ah, the prisoners' list. Nothing.

No official prisoners at present. Senior Witch Yolanda may be held, anyway, at the vizier's home."

They left the school and walked, following the path described in the address book. The island, a dismal, flat place except for the rugged cliffs on the beach, presented an unchanging landscape.

Their destination was not far. Another hole in the ground gaped at them. "We will have to creep in carefully. The occupants are probably asleep, but they may have a sentry," said Jessamine.

The crept down silently, treading each stair with extreme care. Reaching the bottom, they entered a room similar to the school, but smaller. A few doors opened to other rooms, furnished with plain, stone carved furniture. Whatever the vizier did with his incredible wealth, it was not evident here. There was no sign of any life, let alone Aunt Yolanda.

"She is not kept here," said Donna sadly. "It was a wild goose chase."

"We had to know," said Jessamine. She opened the door to look into the last room, and suddenly flew back as if some incredible force punched her in the face. A sooty cloud drifted in. Purple lightening pulsated at its edges, and the sound of thunder rumbled through it. With chilling certainty, Donna recognized the purple face outlined in the cloudy substance. It was the same face she saw when her aunt was abducted. The face grinned viciously with its toothless dark blue mouth, and its hollow, yellow-green eyes winked at Donna, just as it did then. But this time she did not lose her consciousness. Grasping at Bartholomew and Jessamine, she visualized the coordinations of the beach she had used before to transport them to the island. 003-67-8-4. 003-67-8-4. 003- . . .

They were standing on the beach. "Donna, here are the coordinates to my home. 005-98-8-2. Repeat. Transport us."

Donna repeated, but could not continue to concentrate. She saw the purple cloud advancing. It followed them, playing with them, laughing viciously.

"Donna, concentrate!"

She tried. Palms sweating, heart beating. The cloud hovered above them, grinning, obviously enjoying their terror. Without warning, the blue mouth emitted a long, high screech. A small rock at Donna's feet immediately exploded, sending a shower of splinters and torn seaweed around her. Some of the material hit the water. A small whirlpool started to swirl in the dark water. It grew steadily.

"Donna, he started Sound Magic. It will grow. Concentrate on the coordinates or we will die!"

Donna's mind blanked out. Nothing occupied it except the face of the Vizier, mocking her, paralyzing any strength she had left. The whirlpool grew. A huge foam column started forming around it. From a distance, large and small waves, coordinated like advancing soldiers, marched in unison toward the whirlpool. The growing water column fed steadily on the waves. Enormous now, it covered the sky with its swaying bulk. The darkness was torn by purple lightning. The column approached them as if walking on the water, gliding with oily ease.

"Move it, Wicca," screamed Bartholomew, kicking her with his front hoof. "You miserable, cowardly creature. Do you or don't you want to save your aunt?"

Aunt Yolanda's face suddenly filled Donna's mind, replacing the Vizier's terrifying grin. 005-98-8-2. 005-98-8-2. Smiling emerald eyes. 005-98-8-2. Always there, always supporting and loving. 005-98-8-2. 005-98- . . .

They stood at the entrance to Grandmother's tent.

———————

"You can look now, Prime Minister. They are safe."

"Temporarily, Your Majesty. He knows them now."

"It's a chance they had to take, my friend."

"But they failed, Your Majesty."

"I wouldn't say that, Prime Minister. At least we know Senior Witch Yolanda is not kept at the Wizards' School. She must be imprisoned on our planet, therefore, because he has no real power elsewhere, and we have a better chance of saving her."

"True. And he may not think it worthwhile to pursue the girls here."

"Exactly."

"Your Majesty, have you noticed, just before they went, Jessamine said something about our great river having no name . . ."

"Yes. I am ashamed to own that this thought has never crossed my mind, Prime Minister."

Chapter Four

"**I** will never trust you entirely again, Donna," said the camel. "And there is no excuse, no explanation, nothing that could justify your actions, Bartholomew."

"You are upset because you slept through the fun," grumbled the donkey, looking somewhat guilty.

"You jeopardized the mission," retorted the camel.

"We left you the Cinnabar box. The mission was not jeopardized. And Bartholomew came to protect us," said Donna. She had never seen Camellia so angry before. "Please don't be mad, Camellia, please!"

"He should have woken me up – we work as a team. You had no right to go, Donna. Not without consultation. I am truly disappointed in you."

"You were hurt and sick, Camellia," said Jessamine. "You needed rest. We knew you would insist on coming if we woke you up, but someone had to take the Cinnabar box to the queen if something happened to Donna."

"Perhaps. Nevertheless, once I lose my trust"

"Camellia is right," said Grandmother

sternly. "The future of an entire planet is in your hands, Donna. Jessamine, I am surprised. I thought I had instructed you well in Wicca honor."

Jessamine looked up, her black eyes blazing with rage.

"Honor?" she shouted. "Wicca honor? There is no such thing left, Grandmother. We are useless, helpless, miserable worms, dying in the dust, slaves to our fear of the Vizier. Did anyone do anything when my parents were killed? Do you think I will ever forget watching the dam crumbling, dragging them into the filthy water with the Vizier's blue smile hovering in the sky? And do you remember how all of you ran away? Wicca honor indeed. I had a chance to do *something* with Donna. I had a chance to revenge my parents, or perhaps just to save her aunt so that she would not have to suffer the loss like I did . . ." her voice broke and she ran out of the tent into desert.

Grandmother looked helplessly at the tent's flap and at her visitors. She seemed extremely distressed, Donna thought.

"Well, now" said Camellia, batting her long eyelashes to stop her own tears. "Poor little girl. I will go after her immediately. Let's just forget the whole matter, Bartholomew. Donna, darling, I really was so worried – thank goodness you are safe – I must talk to Jessamine – " she spread her large wings and flew off.

Bartholomew laughed. "She can't be angry for more than two minutes at a time," he said affectionately. "Good old Camellia. One wonders how she managed to hate the vizier."

They flew for hours, because settlements were located at great distances, and there was no point in landing in the middle of nowhere. Donna felt drowsy. The swaying motions of the flying camel were much like sitting in a rocking chair during extremely hot weather – uncomfortable but definitely sleep inducing. The drowsiness annoyed her until she was somewhat cheered by the realization that it meant that she was getting used to flying. So she took her belt and tied herself securely to Camellia's neck – just in case.

She woke up with a start as the animals landed in a middle of a deserted little town. The buildings were gray and dusty, made from dry, rotting wood that looked as if it would crumble away any minute. Not a single tree graced the empty, silent streets, and there was no sign of even a small animal to liven it up. The hot wind lifted the dried vegetation and debris from the ground occasionally, and circled it in tiny, dusty whirlwinds. This is really eery, Donna thought. It missed only tumbleweeds to look like a ghost town in some old Western.

"They're gone," whispered Camellia.

"Yup," said Bartholomew. "Probably on their way to the palace."

"Why?" said Donna.

"Their water disappeared," said Bartholomew. "It happens all the time. One night, you go to sleep in a reasonably normal place, for this miserable planet. In the morning you wake up, and the water hole is dry, as if the water was sucked into the ground."

"What do the people do, then?"

"Well, they have a choice – die of thirst or go live like beggars in makeshift towns the queen creates around the palace," explained Bartholomew.

"Not beggars," said Camellia sternly. "Refugees."

"They are starved, thirsty, homeless – show me the big difference, Camellia," said Bartholomew.

"The queen does her best, Bartholomew."

"I know, you stupid old camel. That's not the point – everyone knows how kind the queen is. I just wish she would overlook a few fine points and get things done in a simpler fashion . . ."

"Bartholomew, if she does the things you want her to do she will sink to the level of the evil Vizier. Wicca honor must be upheld."

Bartholomew was quiet for a minute. "No, Camellia. Her concern is grossly exaggerated. She knew for years that the Cinnabar box was in this stupid antique shop. And if she allowed me to steal it, perhaps we could have saved years of agony to the entire planet. The owner would not have even noticed."

"Whether the crime is discovered or not does not matter," said Camellia. "The vibrations of your evil deed would have started a magical chain of events that may have created much worse results. Remember the butterfly fluttering its wings in the forest –"

"If one more person, human or animal, mentions this accursed butterfly fluttering in the forest, I will bray so loudly that you will see a new magical chain of events starting to form. We don't even have forests anymore, for that matter. You may believe all Wicca tales and fantasies if you wish, camel. Just don't expect me to do the same."

"Bartholomew, sometimes I wonder if you are totally loyal to the principles we hold so dear –"

"Will you stop arguing," said Donna wearily. "What are we to do now?"

"Rest in one of the houses until evening, then fly during the night when it's a bit cooler. We have enough water and food for a few days," said Camellia.

"I don't like the look of the place," said Donna. "It looks haunted."

"By what? A few honest ghosts would be a relief after the Vizier's tricks," grumbled Bartholomew.

———————

The house they entered was quiet and dark. The air was cooler, but the closed shutters caused a stifling atmosphere. They spread some blankets on the floor and sat down to eat and rest. Donna felt her eyes closing. Why not sleep for a while, she thought to herself. The animals know what they are doing. They have been agents for so long . . . thousands of years, maybe . . . She fell asleep.

Suddenly she woke up. The room was dark, though she could see through the cracks in the shutters that the sun was shining outside. Am I dreaming? she thought anxiously. She looked around and the animals were not there. She was completely alone. She jumped to her feet, confused and uncertain what to do, and then thought that perhaps they simply went out.

Cautiously, she walked to the door. She walked, and walked, but the door was not any nearer to her. Panicking, she started running toward the door as fast as she could. The door remained the same distance from her as before.

She tried to go to the window at the opposite wall. Again, she could not reach it. The house stretched away from her and she could not get away from its center. Her head started to spin, as if the stretching distances hurt her sense of balance.

Donna tried walking to a third wall that had neither door nor window, and reached it easily in three short steps. It seemed the house was concerned only with keeping her from getting out of doors. She touched the rough boards gingerly with her finger tips, and they felt normal and solid enough. Suddenly the boards waved under her touch, like water, became translucent and shiny for a few minutes, and then solidified into a perfectly clear mirror. She could see her face in it, but the background was not the dark room she was standing in, but the desert, lit by the merciless sun. The donkey and the camel stood there, looking around them, seemingly just as confused as she was. She cried out to them, but they obviously couldn't hear her. She felt sick, terribly nauseated with the dizziness and lack of balance. "Calm down," she said to herself as the sweat beads formed on her forehead and she felt herself trembling. "Sit down. Don't panic. Check resources."

The water bottle strapped to her side was

full. The backpack contained the flat bread and dates that Grandmother gave them for the trip. Donna took a sip of the warm water and felt a little refreshed. Then she stuck her hand to feel the Cinnabar box and it was safe in her pocket. The Wicca locket was on her neck. If only she had some enchantment, she thought helplessly. The Wicca stone. She would have gazed at it, maybe have some sign from Aunt Yolanda . . . She closed her eyes, thinking about her aunt. If all that didn't happen. They would have started their studies, perhaps visited the extinct animal zoo. Life would have been such fun.

The zoo. If only she could go there. She would summon help from the other Witches, or maybe even find Aunt Yolanda, though that was not a strong possibility. Suddenly something occurred to her. The way she took herself, Jessamine and Bartholomew to the other reality was through three steps: gazing at a crystal ball, receiving verbal instruction, and knowing the coordinates. She had none of these advantages, but Aunt Yolanda once said that switching realities was done by a special way of thinking. There may be more than one way to do this thinking.

Coordinates, crystal ball, and verbal instructions. But in the end, it was her own concentration that did it, wasn't it? Well, perhaps if she could give herself the instructions, talk herself into the concentration? Crystal ball. Well, she had a mirror here. This was not an ordinary mirror, either, but something enchanted. If she gazed at the mirror, maybe, just maybe, it would act the same as the crystal ball. Now the coordinates were a complete mystery. But if she visualized a few dodo birds, and a sabertooth tiger, and some dinosaur-like lizards? Wouldn't these images work as coordinates?

But what if it won't work? And worse, what if it works, but she would make a mistake, and go into a reality of a different nature? Well, could it be any worse than being locked in a dark room that could stretch in any direction, probably watched over by the Evil Vizier?

She got up and went to the mirror. The camel and donkey were no longer visible. Concentrating on the mirror, she started talking to herself.

"Donna, visualize a beautiful zoo, without cages. Not a zoo, really, but a natural animal reservation."

A vague, twisting picture formed in the mirror. She jumped with surprise at her immediate success, and the picture was lost.

"Donna, do it again. Without feeling, without any kind of emotion, without surprise."

The picture reappeared.

"Donna, picture a bunch of dodo birds. Then, at a distance, a very great distance, visualize a tiger, all orange. Think about his teeth. Visualize him very, very far."

The picture remained unchanged. She realized that the tiger idea was just too scary, even if she placed him far away. Best to forget the tiger for now and concentrate on the rest.

"Donna, forget the tiger. Just do the dodo birds."

A flock of fat flightless birds appeared in the

mirror. They waddled about and seemed very life-like and natural.

"Donna, bring a prehistoric lizard to this rock on the right side."

A large lizard, sunning itself on the rock with its eyes comfortably closed, gleaming green and purple.

"Donna, project yourself into the picture. Follow the dodo birds' movements. Concentrate. You are there."

Nothing happened. She stood in front of the mirror, looking at the zoo, and could not go there. She had never felt such deep despair. She could not get there without the coordinations – and there was no way to find them. She was going to starve to death in the clutches of the Vizier.

Suddenly, a small movement attracted her attention. Something was forming in the mirror, a small whirlwind, twisting and turning. A small hand, or perhaps a paw, came out of the whirlwind. It waved at her helplessly, and answering its wordless request Donna grasped it firmly. A short struggle, a pull, and suddenly a small animal fell into her arms and gazed at her with large, golden eyes. Even in the middle of a desert in an alien reality there was no possible mistake – she was holding in her arms a small, sleek, fat lemur.

The animal rested its head on Donna shoulder and whined a little. What was the meaning of this? She thought. Why did this animal come out of the mirror when she tried to go to the zoo? The lemur held tightly to her hair. Suddenly she remembered. This had to be Gilbert – her aunt's pet lemur. The fat lemur that lived in the zoo and loved cherry pie.

"Gilbert?" she inquired. The lemur whined again, though this time with great satisfaction, and jumped vigorously on her head. Her courage returned. Whatever the reason for his coming, he somehow managed this, or she managed it for him, without the coordinates – and so she could do it for herself! Shouldering her backpack and blanket, she stepped again in front of the mirror and stared at it. The lemur patted her head rhythmically as if playing a drum.

"Gilbert, stop! I must think. I am going to try getting to the zoo again."

Gilbert obeyed. Again, she visualized the dodo birds, the lizard, and encouraged by the presence of the little animal, even the sabertooth tiger in the distance.

Deeper and deeper. Her eyes hurt, but she avoided blinking, following the instructions originally given by Jessamine. Darkness in the mirror, tiny blinking lights, gray mist –

She stood on a lush, green plain. She had never seen such grass, or such enormous trees. Far away, a sabertooth tiger was sunning himself, and a couple of lizards sat on a nearby rock. But no dodo birds were in sight, and no buildings, no signs of animal reservation, no signs of any life. Gilbert whined. Something was very, very wrong.

Donna had no idea what to do. Since this was not the zoo, it could be anywhere. Another reality, another planet, anything. Most likely, another time, if this was at all possible, because how else could a sabertooth tiger be there? She stood, paralyzed with terror, and waiting for something, anything, to happen, for a long time. But the sun was low in the sky, the air began to cool, and she felt no desire to be eaten by a sabertooth. Something had to be done. She started walking in the opposite direction from the tiger, toward a low range of hills which seemed to be not too far.

"Don't be scared, Gilbert," she said, mostly to encourage herself, as the lemur seemed to take everything calmly in his stride. "I'll try to find a cave or something so we can hide until morning. Then we'll see if we can find a crystal ball, or a mirror, and try to go back to Jessamine's home. I remember the coordinates, I think." The lemur's hold on her hair was comforting.

The hills were farther than she thought, but walking as fast as she could got her nearer to them just at sunset. Strange, though somehow familiar sounds came from that direction.

"If I didn't know better, Gilbert, I would say some people are chanting," she said. The chanting became stronger as she approached the hills. She could see the opening of a cave, with firelight pouring from it. Shadows were moving, dancing, swaying. She crept slowly toward the opening, and peeked in.

About twenty people were dancing around the fire in the middle of a large cave. They wore animal skins, beautifully made into clothes and skillfully embroidered with colorful beads. Two people played the drums, and they played them extremely well, she thought. Any rock group in her world would have been delighted to have them. The people chanted to the rhythm of the drums. The sound waves spread and glided, beautiful and deep and magical. Donna felt herself relaxing, enjoying the soft vibrations of the song. Her fear vanished. She was drawn, without knowing how, into the circle. Moving as if in a dream, she stepped into the amber light of the cave, the lemur holding on to her hair. No one paid any attention to her, and the occupants simply went on dancing and chanting. As if hypnotized, she started to move with them, when a voice, right behind her, stopped her, speaking in an unfamiliar language. She turned around dreamily and smiled blissfully at what seemed like an apparition.

His face was human, but he had large horns adorning his head, seemingly growing from it in a natural fashion. He was covered with golden-brown fur and had a tail, but he stood upright and his hands and feet were much like her own. His eyes were large, sad, and very human.

"I don't understand your language," she said hesitantly.

The creature looked at her and smiled. It was the kindest, sweetest smile she had ever seen.

"But I can speak your language," he said in perfect English, with a gentle, low, musical voice. "I just needed to hear you speak it first."

"Who are you and where am I?" said Donna.

"I am Shape-Changer," said the creature. "In your reality, and your time, they would call me a shaman, but it is too simple a name for me. I am many other things."

"In my time? Is this a different time? Did I do time travel? Does it exist?"

"Yes and no," said Shape-Changer. "It is a different reality from yours, but it's Earth, or rather, another copy of Earth. This is where the extinct zoo will be built, in my future. Our realities, therefore, are forever joined. We are located, using our combined coordinates as a guide, about 30,000 years earlier than where you come from, if I read your thoughts correctly. Of course, to me it seems like the present, even if to you it is the past."

"You read my thoughts?"

"It is part of my talents and my training. Otherwise, I couldn't speak your language."

"I see," said Donna. "I don't like having my thoughts read, though."

"I only read the coordinates and the necessary guideposts. I don't read your innermost thoughts and feelings," said Shape-Changer, "I haven't the slightest wish to intrude."

"Do you know my reality?"

"I know it very well," said Shape-Changer. "I have to. Wicca visitors from all realities always come here, because my people have started it all. Shape changers are the first Wicca, which is why they sometimes call it the Old Religion in your reality. To your people, Wicca is 30,000 years old. I am proud it survived that long."

"So you are a Witch, too . . . why are you called Shape-Changer?"

"I can change myself into animals," answered the creature simply, as if it were an everyday occurrence. Of course, thought Donna, to him it really was a simple matter.

"Why would you do that?"

"To help my people hunt, to protect us from the predators, to create various types of magic, and most important - simply to learn." said Shape-Changer.

"You sound so wise, so educated," said Donna. "And the people are wearing such nice clothes and the music is just great. Funny, I always thought people who lived so long ago were savages."

"And yet your people go to see, and even photograph and print, our cave paintings," said Shape Changer, a smile lighting his sad eyes.

"Cave paintings! Of course! That's why you look so familiar - I have seen your picture in my history book!"

"Yes, there are some really good pictures of me and my relatives in various caves," said the creature modestly. "Did you really believe that savages painted these? Here, come and meet the savages, including one artist. They won't be able to speak your language, since they are all human - usually there is only one shape changer staying with a tribe - but I'll translate. And we are just about to have dinner."

She shook hands all around, the people laughing and trying to talk at the same time, clamoring for Shape-Changer to translate for them. A beautiful steak on a stick, potatoes roasted in the embers of the fire, and a sweet drink made from honey mixed with water would have been marvelous in themselves, but when Donna got an apple, perfectly baked in a clay pot and topped with nuts and berries, she started laughing. Some savages, she thought. How little we know about different realities, different times. How stuck up we are thinking that our computers and fax machines and televisions mean that we are the only civilized people.

One of the women, large and motherly, spread out a soft skin for Donna, gave her another one to use as a blanket, and a few bundled skins to serve as a pillow. The bed was extremely comfortable and as Gilbert curled next to her, she fell asleep almost instantly.

In the middle of the night she woke up suddenly. The fire died, leaving garnet-colored embers. Everything was quiet and hushed, and it was warm and pleasant in the cave. A dark shadow stood sentry in the opening to the cave, his long horns betraying him to be Shape Changer. She stood up, quietly, so as not to wake anyone. Gilbert was snuffling and snorting softly in his sleep, curled into a tight ball.

"Shape-Changer," she whispered, "don't you ever sleep?"

"I sleep a few minutes here and there during the day," said the creature, smiling. "Much like the tigers. I don't need much sleep. I am not like other humans, you know."

"So it's not just the shape changing?"

"It's much more," said Shape-Changer. "In you time, none of us is left. There were never many, anyway. A different branch of evolution, extinct too soon."

"Extinct? Everywhere?"

"Yes, somehow. In every reality I have investigated, we are gone. We were meant to be the Guardians of the Earth. We died out long before your time, and your species failed to do the work properly. Look at the Earth in your reality. Destroyed by ignorance."

"The Witches call themselves Guardians of the Earth."

"Yes, they try. But they don't have our magic, they cannot change shape easily, and they are too few. Also, they have encountered such persecution in their past, many dropped out. The work is immense, Donna. Your planet is sick, very sick. I know who you are, and I know your aunt, Senior Witch Yolanda, the zoo keeper. I know she was kidnaped. And with all my magic, I have no power to help against the evil that took her."

"Why not?"

"Because I am *before* your time in the joint coordinates. In magic, there are many laws and regulations. I can't act in my own future, even in another reality. I can't even retain the future coordinates in my memory."

"Laws and regulations. The people I traveled with talked a lot about it. If I understand correctly, doing an evil deed brings punishment."

"Not punishment exactly, but a chain of events. Like will bring like into existence. And a strong chain of magic, good or evil, will create stronger and stronger events."

"Will you try to help me go back?"

"Of course. But I cannot guarantee success."

"Thank you, Shape-Changer. I wish we had your relatives in my reality."

"We could come back. If you really want us, and try to create the right conditions, we can do what your aunt does for the extinct animal zoo – we can be brought by you, without acting ourselves, into the future. I have talked about it with Senior Witch Yolanda – we can do so much good in your reality. The real problem will be food – we have certain requirements for plants that do not exist in your time."

"Plants! Aunt Yolanda thinks I should specialize in plants in my Wicca studies. Oh, how I hope I can help you come to us, Shape-Changer. I will study so hard, I will do anything. We must, we must find Aunt Yolanda!"

"In the morning, we will go to my place of work and try to get in touch with some of my colleagues. You will love meeting them, anyway."

Chapter Five

Thick vegetation hid the cave opening from view. Shape-Changer moved the vines and Donna squeezed through the narrow entrance into a large, airy chamber. A shaft of light filtered through a crack in the rock ceiling, illuminating the cave with cool, silvery radiance. The light bounced from the clean, dry ground and the large rocks that served as desks, shelves and chairs. Crystals of various sizes and colors, bundles of sticks and twigs, and little leather bags that smelled so good they had to contain herbs, were neatly arranged on the rocks. Donna stared with awe at an egg-shaped, transparent rock crystal. So this is how it all started, she thought. Natural crystals, probably found in streams and lakes. The thought made her realize that this was as close to living the ancient history of Wicca as she could ever get.

"I suppose you use these crystals for your work?" she asked.

"Yes, the stream nearby yields many crystals, well-rounded and polished. I will give you one and teach you how to gaze into it. There is nothing magical about the stones themselves, Donna. It's just how you use them, concentrate on them. You could even gaze into a pool of water and achieve the same results. Nevertheless, I am not sure where you will land in your travels, so you might as well have a serviceable crystal on hand."

He picked the egg-sized crystal and gave it to Donna; it fitted perfectly in the palm of her hand, smooth and comforting. Funny how Wicca tools always felt so right, she thought. The same thing happened when Aunt Yolanda gave her the locket, and even when she first touched the Cinnabar box. "Thank you, Shape-Changer." She said softly. "This will be my crystal if I ever manage to become a true Wicca, and I will keep it forever."

Shape-Changer smiled. She loved to see his rare smile, temporarily removing the sadness from his fathomless dark eyes. Why was he so sad, she thought. Loneliness? Even though he certainly belonged to a different species, his people loved and appreciated him. Too much knowledge of the future? Too much understanding? Perhaps too much responsibility? That must be it. Responsibility can really wear you down . . . She tried to shake off the feeling of her own burden, and managed to fight the tears away.

"Here, you'll need a leather pouch to protect it," said Shape-Changer. She could tell he tried to pretend not to notice her momentary distress. "Now let's go into the inner chamber." They moved deeper into the cave, and entered an immense room through an almost invisible opening in the back wall. The room contained an indoor lake, surrounded by a wide stone ledge. The angle of the light, coming from an unseen source, inflamed the water and the air itself with iridescent, radiant blue tints, as if the entire room was cut from a giant blue jewel. The light darted and danced like a million tiny mice over the water and on the walls.

Shape-Changer took a small flute out of his pouch and started playing a haunting, sweet melody that whispered and echoed like the wind in the reeds of a mountain lake. Donna sat frozen in absolute silence, totally immersed in the sound. Even the lemur didn't move. The music seemed to hypnotize him.

Shape-Changer played for about ten minutes, when suddenly, a bubble floated to the surface of the lake. It looked like a soap bubble, pink and blue and green, and grew slowly and steadily. Something moved inside, or on the surface, Donna couldn't tell with the constantly darting lights. Then, a second bubble popped to the surface and started growing. Shape-Changer played on. The bubbles continued growing and floated a little above the water and back into it, gently bumping into each other.

When each reached the size of a small car, Shape-Changer stopped playing and got up. One bubble drifted onto the ledge and stabilized there. It began to evaporate, to thin out, and suddenly it was no longer there. In its place stood a tall, red-bearded, middle-aged man, dressed like a Viking. His piercing blue eyes matched the cave's light. He seemed immensely strong, not only physically, but as if incredible power emanated from him. Donna sensed these waves of energy enveloping him like electricity.

The Viking said something incomprehensible

to Shape-Changer, looked at Donna thoughtfully, and did an elaborate pattern of movement with his hands, as if conducting an orchestra. When he spoke again, Donna understood every word.

"Shape-Changer, my old friend," said the Viking. "So good to see you. And you too, girl. I see you now understand my speech perfectly. Good."

"Thank you for responding to my call, Vainamoinen," said Shape-Changer. "Donna, meet the grandest Sound Magic wizard of them all. Throughout time, in all realities, there has never been one greater than Vainamoinen. He is from your own reality, born in Finland only a few centuries before your time. People come to him from all over the universe to have him control the oceans and the storms." The Viking bowed and laughed.

"Not exactly," he said. "I assume you called Taliesin as well, and you are just humoring me with these compliments?"

Shape-Changer smiled. "Of course I called him, but I am not humoring you. Taliesin is the master of a different song."

The second bubble evaporated, and a young man, wearing ancient Celtic clothes and carrying a small harp, materialized on the ledge. Donna gasped. She had never seen such a handsome man – not in the movies, not in rock groups, nowhere. He was of middle height, athletic, and as graceful as a cat. Everything about him was perfect – the dark blond hair, the classical features, and the golden tanned skin, almost the same color of his hair. He also looked at Donna and made the same pattern with his hands before starting to talk. His hands were beautiful, strong, and with the long fingers of the musician. She no longer could restrain her curiosity.

"How do you make me understand you?" she asked.

"We rearrange a few sound patterns in your brain," said Vainamoinen. "It won't hurt you, and you will always be able to understand our languages. We could make ourselves understand your language, but we shouldn't, because we come from a reality which is in your past. It's the Wicca Code –"

"More codes, rules, and regulations," said Donna wearily. "So you won't be able to help me, either."

"The Code is essential," said Taliesin, speaking for the first time with a low, magnificent voice that reverberated like music. "Have you ever heard about the butterfly effect?"

"Yes, yes, a million times," said Donna impatiently. "But I worry about my aunt, and a whole planet is drying up, and the vizier is growing more powerful every day, and sometimes you must break a few rules if you want to achieve something!"

"No, not these rules," said Vainamoinen sternly. "Your needs are true and important. But the Vizier thinks his needs are true and important, too. The Code is the only thing that can keep magic under control. Look what happened when the Vizier broke it – a planet was destroyed."

"Allow me to introduce Taliesin," said Shape-Changer. "The greatest singer of all time. His songs move the water, the earth, the fire and the air . . ."

"Stop that, you old fool," said Taliesin,

smiling, teeth flashing white against the golden skin. His eyes were green, a deep dark green like the pine forests. Donna decided she could just see him as the lead singer in a really good band.

"You sing in a group, or solo? What kind of music?" she asked excitedly, for a moment forgetting her troubles.

"No, no, nothing like that, I am a magician. My magic is accomplished with song," explained Taliesin. When he wasn't smiling his eyes expressed infinite sadness, as deep as Shape-Changer's. Why were these powerful beings so depressed, thought Donna irritably. They could achieve so much, but they just stand there and do nothing, with all their stupid rules!

"It's all Sound Magic," said Shape-Changer. "That's why I called these two – they understand the vizier's Sound Magic better than anyone."

"It's really simple," said Vainamoinen. "We, the Finnish magicians, for instance, have power over the oceans. We can ride whalebones instead of ships, and make good time doing it, too. We control the winds and the waves with our song."

"You help sailors?" asked Donna.

"Yes, of course," said Vainamoinen. "When seafaring merchants want to insure a safe trip, they come to us. Any careful, intelligent captain wouldn't take the risk of organizing a trip without some magic. The least he could do is to buy a Wind Rope from a reputable wizard before setting out. He'd hire a magician to go with him, if the trip is really dangerous."

"What's a Wind Rope?"

"It looks like a simple sailor's rope, but the wizard ties three knots in it and sings over them. The knots preserve the original sound waves. During the trip, if the captain needs a steady breeze, he unties the first knot. The second knot produces a strong wind. The captain always hopes he would never have to untie the third knot. Only in a great emergency, such as meeting pirates, he would risk the third knot – and create a violent storm."

"Vainamoinen's power, Donna, is so incredible because his parents were not entirely human but partly entities of air and water," said Shape-Changer. "He controls these elements, as well as the land. His song drives the icy oceans to storms, moves earth, grows plants. Vainamoinen can sing objects that did not exist into being, and make existing objects disappear. He once sang an entire forest to the ground so that his people could grow barley on the land instead."

"And for all my power, Shape-Changer, I cannot help Yolanda," said Vainamoinen, his strong voice suddenly breaking. "Nor can I do anything for Great River." He banged his hand on a rock, so powerfully that Donna expected the rock to split. The rock remained unharmed, but the pain of the blow did not make Vainamoinen even flinch. He turned abruptly and strode out of the cave, and his anger lingered in the cave like a wave of electricity.

"Let me talk to him," said Shape Changer gently. "He is very upset, naturally. But I am sure that when the four of us think calmly together we will find a solution . . ." He turned and followed Vainamoinen.

Donna stared after them, shocked by Vainamoinen's revelation.

"He knows my aunt," she whispered.

Taliesin sat next to her on the ledge and threw a small stone into the water. He watched the rings expanding on the surface silently for a few seconds.

"Vainamoinen and your aunt are great friends, Donna," he finally said. "They met a long time ago, on an expedition they organized to collect sea birds of a species that Vainamoinen was concerned about and Senior Witch Yolanda decided to protect in her zoo. They spend much time together."

"And yet he won't help her."

"He simply can't, Donna. The stronger you are, the more you must observe the rules. It's one thing if a trainee breaks a little rule here and there. But if someone as powerful as Vainamoinen meddles with the Code, the reverberations he unleashes will last for centuries. Think of what the vizier had done! Incidentally, Vainamoinen knows the vizier very well, they studied together on an accursed island where the Vizier now lives –"

"The Wizards' School? Really? I went there to look for my aunt."

Taliesin looked at her with new respect. "You went there? You actually went to the Wizards' School? It's incredibly dangerous."

"I met the Vizier there, and escaped just in time with my friends," said Donna, shuddering with the memory. "He started Sound Magic that created a tornado."

"You have courage," said Taliesin softly. "You will be a great Wicca some day."

"If my aunt survives to teach me," said Donna. She felt tears come into her eyes, softly but irresistibly, and could not stop them. Terror, disappointment, pain, all came together and she sobbed helplessly. Taliesin took her hand gently.

"Cry, Donna. Cry. It will cleanse your heart and make you brave and strong again. Just cry." He held her hand tenderly, looking at her with infinite compassion. She cried until she could no longer cry.

"Donna, if your aunt does not survive, one of us will teach you. We will not allow your talent to go to waste," said Taliesin. "But I am sure she will come back."

"I don't know if I can face it without her, to tell you the truth . . . Taliesin, may I ask you something now? Something sort of personal?" she finally asked, sniffling and exhausted.

"Certainly."

"Why are you so sad? Why is Shape-Changer so sad?"

"Shape-Changer is so sad because he knows about the end of his species. Knowing too much is a great burden. As for me, I am not sure why I am sad. This is my curse, my entire life I have been like that, and I suspect it may be a sickness. Some say it is because of the circumstances of my birth. The legends about my mother and myself are both frightening and sad, and I don't even know if they are true."

"Why don't you ask your mother if the legends are true?"

"I can't. I can't really speak to her, Donna.

She is a wonderful, strong sorceress, but everyone is a little afraid of her, even her own son! I love her and she loves me, but we are not close and we don't talk about things like that."

"Wow," said Donna. "This is exactly the same problem I have with my own mother! Who would have thought that a strong magician like you could have trouble with any relationship?"

"My mother is stronger, I guess. And anyway, you can be a strong Wicca and still remain very human, and sad, and scared, and lonely. I suffer from the sadness all the time. I consulted the healers, but all they suggested was bleeding me or feeding me Belladonna! It's stupid – bleeding makes you weak and Belladonna makes you sleepy, and neither will cure the sadness."

"Belladonna is a poisonous plant," said Donna resolutely. "You shouldn't touch it. And bleeding is so old-fashioned! But of course you are from my past . . . wait a minute. Did any healer suggest St. John's Wort?"

"The little flower? What can it do?"

"In my reality doctors – or healers, as you call them – have recently discovered that it can lift the sadness, or as we call it, depression. As far as I know, no one used this herb in the past."

"How come you know so much about herbal healing, Donna?"

"I just love plants, I guess, and have studied them since I was a little girl. Aunt Yolanda thinks this will be my Wicca specialty."

"Can you get St. John's Wort medicine for me? I really want to try it," said Taliesin enthusiastically.

Donna suddenly laughed, a little bitterly. "Yes, sure, if we meet again. But do you realize I have just prescribed a medication to one of the most powerful wizards of all time? I am nothing next to you, I am nobody, I am not even half-trained."

"You may not be trained yet, but that does not take away your natural talent," said Taliesin. "Why do you have so little confidence in yourself?"

"Because I am ugly," said Donna simply. She couldn't believe she told that to a total stranger, but he already seemed to be an old friend, somehow.

"Ugly? How can you say that?" asked Taliesin, visibly surprised.

"You don't think I am ugly?"

"You still have to grow, of course," said Taliesin thoughtfully, looking at her critically, his head tilted to one side. "You are not quite finished. But do remember, I am a wizard. So I see much more than your current shape – I see your essence, and you are extremely beautiful. There is a song in your essence that is right and true."

"I wish I could see this essence," sighed Donna. "All I know is this image in the mirror, fat and fuzzy-haired, and my complexion is a mess, and I don't like myself in any glasses, no matter how beautiful the frames are, and –"

"Stop," said Taliesin gently. "I see that shape and beauty mean a lot to you. For you, I will break a Wicca rule. A small and harmless one, and it will make you happy. Just don't tell anyone, particularly Vainamoinen. He is so strict!"

From inside his shirt he took a small mirror made of polished metal. "Look into the mirror,

Donna, concentrate and don't blink too much. I will do the rest."

She stared into the mirror. Slowly, an image formed itself in the middle. A young woman sat in the grass, her back toward Donna. She had wonderful, long auburn hair. Donna jumped.

"Aunt Yolanda!"

"No. Look some more, Donna."

The image rotated and Donna saw the woman's face. This was not Aunt Yolanda, but she resembled her a great deal. An incredible, too wonderful to believe sort of suspicion crept into Donna's mind.

"Could this be me in the future? Am I going to look like Aunt Yolanda?" She whispered.

"Allow me to introduce Donna, twenty-one years old," said Taliesin, laughing. "And why wouldn't you resemble your aunt? I saw the family resemblance as soon as I met you."

"Wow," said Donna weakly. "I can't believe this. When does the change take place?"

"What change?" said Taliesin innocently. They both laughed.

"I just have to see myself at different stages," said Donna excitedly. "At twenty-one I have no braces, no glasses, I am slim, my skin seems perfect, my hair is long – and it's auburn! I am in heaven!"

"Well, I rather like your current red hair, but you can have it your way," said Taliesin. "You could start growing your hair now. I can teach you how to bend your mind around little things like overweight and bad skin and correct them. And you should certainly strengthen your eyes – not for beauty, there is nothing ugly about wearing glasses, but for health."

"You could teach me to do that?"

"Absolutely. What is magic? It is the act of controlling reality with one's mind. Nothing is easier than changing your looks - it's your own body, it will easily obey. Much easier than changing a landscape, for instance. Try singing a swamp away sometime! I have to do it all the time for my people, and it's exhausting, believe me. But you wanted to see yourself at various stages. Just direct the ages you want to view into the mirror."

"You could plant Eucalyptus trees to drink away the swamps and save your strength . . . but show me my image at fourteen." The image was slimmer than the way she was at thirteen, no braces, skin much better, hair a little longer, but the same color, glasses still on.

"Sixteen." Good figure, long, darker hair, no glasses, clear skin.

"That's fine," sighed Donna with supreme satisfaction. "I have something to live for." Taliesin laughed.

"You cheer me up even without the St. John's Wort. I can't believe I am actually laughing. I will miss you when you are gone."

"Can't we keep in touch? I do have to bring you the medicine, if everything is all right again," said Donna hesitantly.

"You will have to call me, because I am from your past," said Taliesin. "I will give you my coordinates, and then you can visit whenever you want."

"Only if you tell me that it's all right, Mr.

Taliesin."

"Mr.? Oh. No, don't call me that! It's traditional to call wizards by their first name, without glorification. Besides, you let me call you by your name, without a title. I don't call you Lady Donna."

"But you are so important, and older than me."

"How old are you?"

"Thirteen."

"Then I am not that much older. I am seventeen, in my reality, and I don't consider myself important. And you, perhaps, may cure me of my curse of sadness, so you are my friend. Doesn't that make you just as important?"

"Well, maybe a little bit . . . but there is something else . . . well . . . you are so very handsome, you know . . ."

"Ah. Shape and beauty again. Who cares? I am a shape changer, remember? The body is less important to me than the soul. Does it really make a difference?"

"Sort of. It's like being a groupie. Do you know what a groupie is? It's someone who follows rock stars everywhere. I don't like acting like that."

"I am not sure I understand how rock stars and groupies behave. But I do know we can be great friends. You seem to understand the sadness, and talking to you makes me feel good."

"Can you tell me this awful legend, or is it too private, Taliesin?"

"I can tell you. Everyone knows it in Wales, where I come from. Before I was born, my mother gave birth to an incredibly ugly son. I don't know the details, but they say he was half man, half animal, maybe with a pig's snout. She wished to give him happiness by making him wise. Using various herbs, she created a special potion that would give him incredible wisdom. Unfortunately, a young assistant magician tricked her and drank the potion himself. Mother chased the thief for days. He made himself extremely clever by drinking this potion, and both of them were expert shape-changers, so the chase was fast and furious. They constantly changed, taking the shapes of various animals or plants. Finally, he found a heap of barley, turned himself into a single grain and mixed with the rest. But there was no escape – Mother was just too good. She saw which grain was really the young magician, turned into a bird and ate the grain.

So now she carried the magic seed inside her. When she turned back into a woman, she realized she was pregnant – the seed turned into a baby. She swore to kill it as soon as it was born, because she felt it may revive the vicious assistant as her son. But instead, they say she gave birth to a boy so beautiful, so glowing and sweet, that she could not keep her vow. I guess I was a cute baby, despite being born of magic and pain. Unlike the dishonest assistant magician I replaced, I try to be good and faithful, and I am loved by my people and obeyed by the elements. But I carry this pain with me forever. I have never sung any song of joy."

"Well, I can see why you can't ask your mother about it. I wouldn't dare to ask my mother, either. There are so many parts of this legend that are really scary. But still, maybe it's just a story, and I don't see why you should pay such a high price, even if it were true. You did nothing wrong – all that stuff happened before you were born! So I'll find you some St. John's Wort, and I must say, in my century we have a marvelous new collection of other herbs and things that will help you, Taliesin. And then you can write some happy songs. I really want to hear you sing, anyway."

"Great. Here, I will write my coordinates for you on this piece of leather. When all of this is over, we will absolutely and certainly meet, and I will be happy to sing for you. Maybe, just maybe, in time I can do some songs of joy. I want to so much . . ."

"Say," said Donna, trying to divert him. "Just for fun, show me how you do shape-changing."

Taliesin laughed. "All right," he said, and disappeared. Next to her sat a lemur, resembling Gilbert in every detail. Donna jumped, and the real Gilbert leapt off her shoulder and stared at the newcomer with deep suspicion. The two lemurs started prowling around each other, and in a few seconds Donna could not tell the difference. She stood, gaping in disbelief, as Vainamoinen and Shape-Changer returned to the cave. Vainamoinen glared at the two lemurs. His air of controlled resolution scared Donna a little and he sensed it.

"Don't be afraid of me, girl," he said gruffly. "I am sorry for my behavior. Standing aside and letting others take the danger is destroying me, and yet I must obey the Code."

"I understand," said Donna. "Taliesin explained the Code to me and I am beginning to see what you mean, Mr. Vainamoinen – I mean Vainamoinen – he also said I should call you by your first name only."

The wizard laughed. "Yes, we are so proud that we pretend to be humble, ah, Shape-Changer? Never mind. We did think about something while Taliesin spent his time turning into a small beast!"

"He was very helpful, actually," said Donna loyally. "There is so much I understand better now . . ."

Vainamoinen laughed. "Children will be children, as we say in Finland! Shape-Changer told me that you had been separated from two flying animals, and that the Vizier put them in a desert environment that you saw at this funny house at Great River. I think I know where he took them."

"You mean he removed them from Great River altogether? But why would he do that?"

"You see, the Vizier's birth place is a reality called Borderland, a place where magic is commonplace. Not very strong magic since it is spread out too thinly, but this is where he had started his studies, of course, and where he has many friends. Also, various animals of magical nature exist in Borderland, so it would be easy to take your friends there without attracting much attention."

"Is this where Camellia and Bartholomew were born? I saw no other flying beasts in Great River."

"Very likely. The Vizier probably sent them back there to be jailed by some of his spies. I think he does not dare to kill them, because despite his command over Great River and its queen, he knows that if any of us becomes angry enough to break the Code he will be finished. When he abducted Yolanda, I was close to doing exactly that. I could eliminate him with such ease . . ." he clenched his fists.

"Can't I go with Donna?" said one of the two lemurs seriously. "I have been to Borderland, you know –"

"Don't be stupid, my boy," said Vainamoinen, kindly. "Who are you trying to cheat? The Code can't be changed. You may go to Borderland when someone from their reality summons you, and stay the prescribed time. You know that."

"Will you at least let me sing into her crystal?"

"We both will," Said Vainamoinen. "Can't be too careful. But will you please change back into your normal self? Donna, hand me your crystal. We will make this crystal very easy to use, so easy, in fact, that you will not even need coordinates to get from one reality to another."

She took the crystal out of its pouch and put it on a rock between them. Taliesin resumed his shape, touched the strings or his harp, and burst into a song. His magnificent voice swelled like waves into air and water and stone. Vainamoinen began producing a sound that combined the sighing of the wind, the call of sea birds, and the twinkling of raindrops on water. Their sounds merged, expanded, rolled. Space seemed to disappear, only the music remained. Mist and rain from Taliesin's land, wind and snow from Vainamoinen's filled the air, enveloping Donna with coolness and grayness and song. Time stood still. The universe contained nothing but the glorious sound. Then unexpectedly it stopped, and she came back to reality, confused and disoriented.

The crystal changed colors. It turned smoky and slightly warmer to the touch.

"You will use it to view and join your animal friends, as soon as you get to Borderland," said Vainamoinen.

"You will meet strange animals there," said Taliesin. "Don't be frightened of them. It's just their shape, and I hope I have convinced you that shape matters less than you think. Many of them are extremely kind. Beware of the humans, though. Some of them are not too honest."

"Are they terribly dangerous?" Asked Donna.

Taliesin sighed. "I wish I could go with you. You have no idea how much I wish I could protect you."

"Don't scare the little Wicca, my boy," said Vainamoinen. "She has to do it. There is no other way. And like her aunt, she has courage, right, girl?"

"I hope so, Vainamoinen. I must find Aunt Yolanda."

"Yes, girl. Find her, find her. The world without that Witch is just not the same –"

"Time to go, Donna," interrupted Shape-Changer abruptly, as usual sensing how she felt. "You will find your animal friends there, and the three of you will go back to Great River and complete your mission. All will be well."

"Can you talk me through it? It's easier this way," she said, shouldering her backpack and picking up Gilbert. "Good bye, Vainamoinen. I will find Aunt Yolanda. Good bye, Shape-Changer. I know we will meet again soon. Aunt Yolanda will find a way to help your people. Good bye, Taliesin. I will bring you the medicine, some day, I promise." Her voice broke a little and she hugged Gilbert tightly. "Thank you for everything, all of you."

"Donna, gaze at the crystal," said Shape-Changer quietly.

Remembering not to blink, she gazed.

"Donna, imagine a desert. Imagine a beautiful, colorful desert, not like Great River."

Red sky over golden sand. Marvelous palm trees in a gigantic oasis. Tents made of purple and blue material. Horses, camels, people wearing exotic clothes and golden jewelry.

"Donna, imagine a sea. Blue and shining."

Sapphire sea. High waves, crested with white foam with green, turbulent stripes. White sandy beach.

"Donna, imagine beautiful flowers. Lilies, roses, jasmines, carnations. Lush gardens, well kept, lovely orchards, full of fruit."

A huge rose garden, bordered by immense orange trees, the fragrances mingling in the warm air, born on a soft breeze.

"Donna, the name is written in the crystal. Repeat the name. Borderland."

Borderland.

She swayed, lost her balance and Gilbert held tightly to her hair as the hot, humid wind slapped her face and the brilliant light overwhelmed her eyes.

Chapter Six

Donna stood in the midst of a large crowd of people, on a reddish dirt road as wide as two big city avenues put together. On one side of the road stretched a brilliant sapphire sea, on the other side, saffron-yellow cliffs, as tall as skyscrapers, gleaming against the bright cerulean-blue sky. The scene was bathed in a light so intense, so golden, that everything stood out in a sharp contrast and almost without shadows. Donna rubbed her eyes as they smarted in the sudden brilliance and oppressive heat.

No one paid attention to her despite the fact that she balanced a lemur on her head, probably because most people on this road presented an even stranger image. They wore varied outfits. Long embroidered robes and giant feather head dresses, Medieval suits of armor, white draperies that vaguely reminded Donna of Ancient Greece, khaki military uniforms and hats that could imply the French Foreign Legion but not exactly – she couldn't really identify any of them. Many animals strolled along as well. The fake Legionnaires swayed on camels, the Medieval knights rode magnificent horses, and a few children sat in elaborate wicker structures mounted on a procession of elephants. Small herds of sheep and goats wandered everywhere, some of them ridden by monkeys wearing smart red and gold uniforms decorated with large tassels on their shoulders. One woman held a cheetah-like animal on a golden leash, but the creature had an almost human face. It grinned at Donna as it slithered along, showing sharp, yellow teeth. Five large, white, elegant Afghan hounds, each with a single horn on its head like a mythological unicorn, followed a man dressed in an old Russian outfit, complete with a tall fur hat, leather boots, and a fur-lined robe. Donna wondered how he could stand the heat.

The wide road allowed everyone to walk or ride comfortably in both directions, without any crowding or haste. The complete absence of wheeled vehicles probably helped. Nevertheless, since everyone walked more or less purposely, Donna felt that standing still might attract attention, so she fell in with the crowd and started walking. Gilbert tapped her head nervously with both paws, glared at a passing zebra and made threatening sounds like a small dog. "Stop, Gilbert," said Donna, nervous herself. "No use alerting the inhabitants –" when she suddenly realized that the zebra had wings, neatly folded on each side of its back and supporting the rider, a mysterious person completely shrouded in black veils.

The winged zebra reminded her to check on flying animals. Lifting her eyes to the sky involved effort because of the extremely strong light, but she shaded her eyes with her hands and attempted it.

The sky was full of unidentifiable flying objects. If Camellia and Bartholomew flew there, they were lost in a crowd of their own.

The road seemed to stretch forever. However, smaller roads connected to it occasionally, and people got off the main road to follow them. These secondary roads wound in such a circular way as to prevent Donna from seeing where they led, but invariably they turned away from the sea. The wide, deserted beach, therefore, presented a good place for resting. It would give her the privacy to gaze into her crystal and try to connect with Camellia and Bartholomew.

She settled on the soft sand under a small cliff that hid her from the multitude on the road. Gilbert climbed down into her lap and tapped the backpack, so she gave him food and water and drank some herself, the extreme heat preventing her from feeling any hunger. Looking around, she noticed that small trees, not much bigger than bushes, grew directly in the sea. Intrigued, she walked to examine one of them, as she knew that most trees cannot survive the large content of salt usually present in sea water.

It had gray bark and contorted branches, covered with conifer-like foliage. Yellowish-green gourds, the size of a large watermelon, hung limply over the waves. She touched one of them gingerly, and to her surprise it began to move and shake gently. Shaking faster and faster, it suddenly cracked open. White, fluffy, silky material lined the inside, supporting the plump, red-green body of a small duck and firmly attached to its bill. The duck hung on for about five minutes, drying its feathers in the strong sun and flapping its wings vigorously. Then it let go of the gourd's lining, dropped with a thud into the sea and expertly swam away. Another fruit started shaking.

Well, she thought, shrugging her shoulders, they told you the place crawled with magical animals, but still, a duck tree! Botany would never feel the same. She came back to Gilbert and was about to take the crystal out and start gazing, when she suddenly noticed a movement in the brilliant sky high above her. Something, or someone, flew above her, and for a moment she dared to hope that perhaps Camellia and Bartholomew somehow knew she sat on the beach. However, she observed five objects in the sky, and much too large, even at this distance.

The objects descended slowly and leisurely, and after a few minutes became easier to see. Five flying carpets, each supporting two or three women, hovered above Donna. She rubbed her eyes, but the things just stayed there, hovering. Well, she thought, if flying camels, why not flying carpets? The carpets bobbed and settled around her precisely and delicately.

The women wore costumes that came straight from the stories of the Arabian Nights. Silk and jewels and gold from head to toe, tassels and embroidery and shawls and pointed shoes, the colors giving Donna a headache. "Welcome," said one of the women sweetly. "Welcome to Borderland. We offer you hospitality and would like you to come and stay at the palace."

"How did you know I came here?" Asked

Donna. She no longer even questioned the queer fact that she understood every language in these insane realities.

"My husband saw you in his crystal ball," said the woman. "I am the wife of the Vizier –"

"The Vizier!" screamed Donna and jumped to her feet. "No way, I'm not going!"

"Oh, I am sorry, my dear. I did not mean the Evil Vizier of Great River. My husband is Jaafar, Vizier to the great Haroun-al-Rashid, blessed be his name, our magnificent and benevolent Calif . . ."

"Oh, sorry," interrupted Donna. "I didn't mean to be rude. But you know Great River –"

"Everyone knows about the unhappy place, and I have special reasons to hate the Evil Vizier," sighed the woman and touched her eyes with an embroidered silk handkerchief, permitting clouds of perfume to float around her. Donna sneezed. "Come, my dear, sit on the carpet and let's go to the palace."

Donna sat on the carpet, with Gilbert attaching himself as usual to her hair. Everyone else climbed on. Since no one tied herself to the carpets, Donna did not want to question their mode of traveling, but this was even worse than riding the flying animals. Nothing stood between her and a horrible fall, and she didn't trust the power that propelled the carpets as much as she trusted Camellia's and Bartholomew's natural wings. She had to admit, though, that those carpets were pretty steady, and the pleasant sea breeze didn't make them wobble. I am getting used to this, she thought wearily, but I am glad that Aunt Yolanda told me that witches don't really ride brooms - I draw the line on flying on a miserable, skinny broom - and she opened her eyes, tightly shut throughout the trip, only as the carpet hit solid ground.

The entire palace was made of marble, astonishingly white against the strong blue and gold of the landscape. The palace stood partially on the beach, with the main gate opening on it, and partially inside the sea, with broad marble stairs descending directly from the back gate into the water. The water played on the stairs with an endless array of tiny waves and darting lights, and a few mermaids sat on them, waving their silvery tails in the water and throwing food at a herd of squirrel-size seahorses that played around them. Donna noticed that the mermaids had human upper bodies and long flowing hair, but their faces were not human. Rather, they looked very much like a manatee, an animal she particularly liked. One of them held a baby that looked like a living toy. Funny, she thought. All the mythology books said that sailors thought they saw mermaids when they came across manatees. In this reality, they saw both at the same time!

Attendants rushed over to roll the carpets and take them away, and the women strolled into the palace. The sudden coolness and darkness almost shocked Donna. Air-condition units, she thought, couldn't possibly be the answer in a place like that, so it had to be magic. Then she noticed the small windows, covered with lattice-work with many climbing plants, thus admitting pleasant, green light. She suddenly remembered reading about various ancient cultures on Earth that had built stone houses that remained completely cool in the most arid, hot regions. It didn't require magic – only natural resources such as heavy, thick stone walls, strategically placed small windows, and intelligent use of plants and water. In a way, she thought, respecting the environment is magic, too, and Witches are truly the Guardians of the Earth, after all. Suddenly, for the first time, she felt proud to be a Wicca. Some day I'll teach people how to use plants properly in such buildings and we won't need to waste so much energy on cooling thin, uncomfortable, expensive houses like the one Mom and I lived in, she thought. Houses and cities full of plants, full of life, friendly to the Earth and the animals.

The large hall and the drawing room it led to, were also polished marble, ceiling, walls, floor, all white. However, wine-red carpets, furniture made of dark rosewood, and many bright copper and brass decorations created an atmosphere of supreme opulence. And white flowers everywhere. Translucent porcelain vases full of lilies and roses, brass pots planted with climbing jasmines, and miniature flowering citrus trees and plumerias shone in every corner like little fragrant stars.

The Vizier's wife clapped her hands and almost immediately an attendant brought a tray laden with refreshments, then floated away just as quickly. The other women also left and Donna remained alone with her hostess, who leaned back on a divan covered with cushions and motioned Donna to a second one. She picked up a large fan made of peacock feathers.

"I have not introduced myself. My name is Helena," she said. "Please have some pomegranate juice, you must be thirsty in this terrible heat. Oh, I'll never get used to such heat. It's so different in my country, Iskandar." She handed Donna a tall crystal glass full of ruby-red liquid. Donna drank. A pleasant, thirst-quenching drink despite the excessive sweetness, she thought. She took a small triangular cake, made of many sheets of dough and drenched in sweet-smelling rose water and honey.

"This is wonderful," she said to her hostess.

"Baklava," said Helena, "but different. They don't know how to bake it here! I sent for the recipe from my country, after I was released from enchantment, since no one cooks like the chefs of Iskandar."

"You were released from enchantment?" asked Donna curiously.

"Well, yes, both my lady and I were bewitched by the Evil Vizier centuries ago, when he was young and still living in Borderland. I am still humiliated by the memories."

"You are a few centuries old? You look so young!" said Donna, astonished.

"Thank you," said the lady, pleased. "Yes, I am four-hundred and sixteen years old. That's not really old, you know. Most of us, human or animal, live very long in this reality –"

"That settles it," interrupted Donna jubilantly. "My flying animals are about four thousand years old. So, I am sure they were born here, and the Vizier must have jailed them here. But can you tell me a little about the enchantment?"

"I would, but I am afraid you will hold it against me . . ."

"No, never, I know that the Vizier hurt so many people," said Donna. She burned with curiosity.

"He turned us into owls," said the lady, and hid her face behind her fan. She looked up again, scarlet with embarrassment. "Screeching owls, can you imagine? And just because my lady would not marry him. Who would? Nasty creature that he was even then, and she the daughter of the King of Iskandar . . . why should she marry that lout?"

"Then what's to be embarrassed about? It wasn't your fault!"

"But screeching owls! We actually screeched! And some people tell us, whenever we argue with them, that we still screech!"

"Well, I am sure these people deserve some screeching every so often," said Donna sympathetically. "Most people do. And who is your lady?"

"She is my darling cousin Fatima, now the wife of Haroun-al-Rashid. She and I were brought up together like sisters. Haroun and Jaafar had a habit, then, of going amongst the people in disguise. They claim they did it because they wanted to know how their subjects really lived, and truly understand them and relate to them. Well, Fatima and I think they were just looking for fun and adventures, and you may be sure we stopped this ridiculous custom as soon as we married them a long time ago, let's see - this will be my one hundred and ninety seventh anniversary coming next winter. Anyway, the Evil Vizier turned them into a pair of storks, for some reason they never quite figured out (or just didn't want to tell us), and they wandered on to the lonely tower where Fatima and I were imprisoned. Since we knew a little magic, we helped them recover the formula and return to their former shape."

"If you knew magic, why didn't you release yourselves?"

"It's not so simple. Everyone here knows a little magic, but the Vizier's magic was much stronger, even then. He really knew his business. However, when you combine certain elements, such as helping someone else in trouble, there are many tricks. Of course, Haroun and Jaafar had to promise to marry us as soon as they became human, and this presented a bit of a problem."

"Why wouldn't they want to marry you? Such a wonderful romantic way to find wives! Wow, just like in the stories, princesses locked in an enchanted tower . . ."

"Because we couldn't tell them who we were, what we really looked like, or anything. You see, this is a part of the Code of enchantment in these cases, the release has to be done on faith and rewarded by keeping a difficult promise. And we did look awful, two human-size owls dressed in white veils and golden jewelry! You can bet Jaafar and Haroun fretted – I really ought to remember to refer to him as Haroun the Magnificent Blessed Calif or something – but they had no choice. And once they married us, the owl shapes dissipated and they realized they married the daughter of the King of Iskandar and her first cousin. So they were well pleased with the outcome after all."

"If Mrs. Calif is half as nice as you, then both

the Calif and Jaafar are lucky," said Donna truthfully and took another Baklava. "To think that they had hesitated marrying you! How could they be so awful – well, they deserve all the screeching in the world!" Helena laughed. "So you guessed who talks about screeching! Thank you, how kind you are. But unfortunately, not everyone in Borderland feels the same about Fatima and me. Some hate the Calif anyway. Some love the Calif but think he should have married a local woman. Most of the enemies who talk about us are spies for the Evil Vizier, of course, and both Haroun and Jaafar are worried. Oh, I think Jaafar is coming."

A tall, elegant man in plain blue robes entered the room. He had a black, pointed beard and black eyes, and his one ornament was a large seal ring. Donna liked his pleasant, straightforward smile. "Well, well, so this is the little Wicca from Earth," said Jaafar. "Pleased to meet you."

"It's funny," said Donna. "You appear in those Arabian tales I have read since I was a baby. I know that Haroun-Al-Rashid existed in my reality, and had a Vizier by the name of Jaafar. I always thought the stories were written about them. And yet both of you are here in person in Borderland. I just don't get it."

"Just the normal mixing of realities," said Jaafar and took a glass of pomegranate juice. "Yes, a Calif by that name once lived in your reality, though a very different person from the one living here. The tales about our Calif seeped from this reality into yours, and as the names were the same, naturally settled on your Calif. I am not sure if a Jaafar ever existed in your reality. It happens often, you know. Many folktales and mythologies in various realities are the history of some other reality. Of course, I will take you to meet the Calif and the queen as soon as you are ready."

"She must rest, Jaafar. This heat! I will take her to her room and she can meet them at dinner. Look at your pet, Donna. He loves the baklavas."

"Gilbert is addicted to sweets," said Donna. She grabbed him before he landed in the middle of the tray, and served him a piece of baklava in a more respectable manner. Jaafar laughed and petted the lemur's head.

Donna had never seen such a bedroom. Gold and crimson damask covered a four-poster bed, draped with a gauzy white net. Oriental rugs, woven with endless tiny flowers and arabesques covered the white marble floor, and soft cushions were scattered everywhere. Alabaster bowls full of peaches, plums, and persimmons, and vases of tall, crimson roses stood on small tables that were inlaid with precious woods and mother of pearl. I wish I were in my little room at Aunt Yolanda's new house, she thought sadly, overwhelmed by the cloying luxury of this palace. Depressed and exhausted, she kicked off her shoes, threw herself on the golden bed and fell asleep.

After about an hour she woke up, feeling more cheerful. To her surprise, she found a green embroidered robe, underwear, and lovely brown leather sandals, all arranged neatly on a low chair near the bed. On a little table next to it stood a pot of hot chocolate and a fragile porcelain cup. She poured herself some and drank it, grateful for the coolness of the palace that allowed drinking such a hot beverage with comfort, and went exploring for a bathroom. She didn't want to put on these marvelous clothes without a good shower. The first door she opened, however, led into a garden as large as a football field. Nearby stood five or six small trees, very much like the duck trees she saw at the beach. An old woman, perched on a stool, clipped away some yellow foliage with gardening shears. The woman smiled at her. "Are you interested in plants?" she asked.

"Yes, very much," said Donna. "I saw a similar tree growing in the sea, and the fruit produced a duck."

"These are Baromez trees," said the woman proudly. "Lady Helena brought them from the land of the Tartars, near her homeland of Iskandar. Absolutely the best Baromez in the world. Superb wool, silky and warm, and it's much sought after."

"Wool?" said Donna. "Wool grows on sheep, not on trees, I always thought." She watched the large gourds suspiciously, already having a hunch that the ducks were simple by comparison.

"So you don't know the Baromez," answered the woman, smiling. "Watch. I will touch one of the ripe gourds, and look what happens."

The gourd began to shake just like the duck gourd. Suddenly, it burst open, and a brown, tiny lamb jumped out of it. It seemed to be attached to the fruit by a long umbilical cord, and stood there on its tiny legs, shivering and whimpering helplessly.

"Poor darlings, they can't free themselves from the tree," said the woman. "We, the gardeners, must release them." Gently, she loosened the cord and took out a jar of medicine and a clean bandage from a small burlap sack that hung from her belt. She put the medicine on the lamb, wrapped the bandage around its little stomach, then fished a baby bottle out of the sack.

"Would you like to feed the Baromez?" she asked, handing Donna the bottle.

Donna took the tiny soft animal and cradled it in her arms. She put the bottle in its mouth and it sucked happily like any baby enjoying its first good meal.

"We have a lovely herd," said the old woman. "They live in a comfortable, large enclosure, and we cut their wool every year and sell it for a fortune." The Baromez finished the milk with amazing speed, and the bottle fell out of its mouth.

"Now, Malka, you are wasting our guest's time," said a gravely voice near Donna.

"No, no, I love it," said Donna, unable to take her eyes off the tiny Baromez, now fast asleep and snuffling her arm gently with its warm snout.

"Nevertheless, you must get ready for your audience with the Calif," said the person insistently. Donna looked up and saw no one. Confused, she looked around. "I am here, by your feet," said the voice, obviously amused.

A toad stood there, as tall as Donna's knee. She wore a purple velvet dress, and silver bells decorated her feet. The little horns on her head had jewels around them, suggesting earnings. The toad bowed.

"My lady, I am Roxanne, your attendant while you stay at the palace," said the toad.

"Pleased to meet you, Roxanne. Just call me Donna."

"Thank you. Would you please step inside? It's time for your bath."

I am either totally immune to surprises now, thought Donna, or I have lost my mind. Well, if a lamb tree, why not a well-dressed toad? She followed Roxanne into the luxurious bathroom.

"Care for some music while you get ready?" asked the toad courteously. "You know, we toads are famous for our playing and our dancing." Anyone who loved music couldn't be all bad, thought Donna. "Sure," she said. "Do you play an instrument, too? And you have an interesting voice. I bet you sing."

"Why, yes, of course, most toads do," said Roxanne. "We are often hired precisely for this talent." She produced a small balalaika, beautifully made from inlaid wood and ivory, and plucked the strings expertly to see if the instrument was properly tuned. She adjusted them slightly and burst into a song. Her voice was surprisingly strong for such a small creature, and very appealing, Donna thought.

Lying in the huge tub filled with scented warm water and rose petals, a glass of lemonade by her side and the toad singing emotionally uplifting Russian-Gypsy ballads, wasn't so bad after all. Perhaps, thought Donna, one can get used to a little luxury, under the right circumstances. Maybe. As long as it doesn't take place in a country club, of course.

She found the long robe hard to manage, but her shorts and T-shirt were certainly inappropriate for dinner with Haroun-al-Rashid. Anyway, Roxanne washed them nicely and at the moment they were dripping into the elegant marble bathtub in Donna's bathroom. When she walked into the dining room with Gilbert riding her shoulder, she was glad to be beautifully dressed.

The room contained a table which could sit a hundred people or so. It seemed to stretch for miles, covered with gold utensils and porcelain plates and decorated with vases of white roses and heavy gold candle sticks. Only a few of the candles were lit, though, and the magnificent room hid itself in half shadow. A small group of people stood at the open window, overlooking the garden. One man detached himself from the group and came to meet her, smiling, hand outstretched. A small black cat rode his shoulder.

Silently, Donna shook the hand of the great Calif, a figure of history and legend, a storybook character from her childhood. He was a middle-aged man, with a tanned face and black hair and beard, touched with gray. His chocolate-brown, kind eyes smiled at her. "I am Haroun-al-Rashid. Don't look so awed, my child. I am only a king who lives for his people. The good wizards you have met are so much greater than I am because they are the Guardians of Wisdom."

"I am honored to meet you, Your Majesty,"

said Donna, finding her voice. This was the sentence Roxanne taught her. The Calif laughed. "Come, meet my wife," he said. "You have already met Jaafar and Helena. We will have dinner, just the five of us, and discuss what can be done. I am not sure how to help you, but you know I will do my very best."

"I hope it is all right that I brought my lemur," mumbled Donna. "He was afraid to stay alone in my room . . ."

"Your lemur is welcome. As you can see, I love animals," said the Calif, stroking the little black cat that snuggled comfortably on his broad shoulder. "Anyway, dinner today is a private affair. We have no time to lose."

It's amazing, thought Donna, how all these grown-ups, some of them powerful and even intimidating, had no power against the Vizier. Either they had this annoying Code to attend to, or they had no idea what to do. If she expected miracles from Haroun-al-Rashid, they were not available. The Calif did not know Aunt Yolanda's whereabouts, though common gossip about the abducted Senior Witch did reach Fatima's ears. Nor did any of them know Camellia or Bartholomew personally, though they were aware of these animals going into service with the queen of Great River centuries ago. Fatima knew the queen before Great River became desert, but had not seen her for centuries.

Donna pulled out the crystal and explained the extra magic done to it by Vainamoinen and Taliesin, both well known at Borderland. As soon as dinner was over, they sat around it and gazed together, as Fatima and Helena had experience in crystal gazing since childhood.

In an instant, the image of Bartholomew and Camellia came into the crystal. They seemed to sit in a cave, at any rate in a rocky environment, huddled to each other, quiet and subdued. Donna cried out, dismayed, "They are imprisoned, I can see that!"

"Yes, so it seems," said Jaafar, stroking his beard and thinking deeply. "I think I can tell where they are by the look of these rocks. The desert, of course. Where else would he hide them?"

"So what shall we do?" said Fatima.

"Tomorrow morning, first light, we will send many soldiers on flying carpets to this area. We will look everywhere. It's about three or four hours flight, if I am correct about the location. I will come too, of course. Now, try to concentrate on gazing on the environment."

It certainly looked like a desert, though not at all like the desert of Great River. A large mountain, with many caves dotting it all over. In front of it, a camp surrounding a large water hole. Purple and blue tents, many camels and horses, large palm trees. A beautiful red sky at sunset.

"Yes, it seems like the kind of place where the Vizier would settle some of his spies, to live in comfort," said Haroun-al-Rashid.

"Could he keep Aunt Yolanda there as well, do you think?" said Donna, not really daring to hope.

"I don't know," said the Calif. "The Vizier is very subtle. He hides himself behind a thousand illusions. I have defeated jinns and demons in my time, but nothing like him."

———

In the middle of the night Donna suddenly woke up. "Psst, Wicca," she heard a hissing voice. "Wicca, wake up."

She sat up in bed. Outside her window stood a large deer with beautifully branched horns. As she stepped to the window, she noticed that the animal had large wings, much like Camellia and Bartholomew.

"I am Peryton," said the creature. "I came to take you to Camellia and Bartholomew."

"But the Calif wants me to go in the morning with his soldiers," said Donna.

"Don't believe him, Wicca. He just wants to lure you to the desert so that he could kill you unobserved by the animals. All humans here are slaves to the Evil Vizier. Only the animals are trustworthy."

Donna hesitated. She remembered what Taliesin said – most of the animals were trustworthy but strangely shaped. Many humans were not to be trusted. But the Calif and his friends seemed so concerned, so kind.

"Why do you hesitate, Wicca? Don't you realize the truth?"

"What are you talking about? What truth?"

"And you call yourself Wicca," said the creature disdainfully. "Don't you realize that Jaafar is the Evil Vizier, and that Haroun-al-Rashid is really his servant?"

Donna gaped at the creature. This, of course, could be true. The Evil Vizier was an expert in illusion. What would be simpler than to assume the form of the loyal Jaafar, marry the Calif's sister-in-law . . . He took service with the queen of Great River in just the same way, after all, and then became a renegade. What should she do? Well, if she goes, and if Peryton is lying, the Calif simply will send his troops in the morning to complete the mission. And if Peryton told the truth, then escape seemed necessary. Suddenly she had an idea. "All right," she said. "Just let me get dressed and take my stuff, and get my lemur." She really had no choice. But there was one little thing she could do, though, before going. Just in case.

Chapter Seven

They flew silently, speedily, Peryton's powerful wings seemingly tireless. When the sun rose, Donna saw the luxurious camp she had gazed at in the crystal the night before. Peryton started the long descent, and soon the earth came nearer and the glorious sunrise gleamed behind. Then Donna saw something that simply could not be. Peryton's shadow, strongly delineated on the white sand, was not the shadow of a winged deer. Instead, Peryton cast the shadow of a man. She stepped away a little, suspecting some visual illusion created by mixing her own shadow with his. It didn't help. The human shadow remained. What could this mean?

Peryton turned his head at her and laughed. Somehow his voice sounded not only hissing but vicious. "Ah," he said, coldly amused. "So you noticed already? I hoped you wouldn't until the Vizier came by."

"I see," said Donna calmly, hiding the mounting terror. "A human shadow. You are not really one of the animals, are you?"

"I am Peryton," said the deer. "I told you the truth. And if you were better educated, you ignorant, stupid Wicca, you would have known what it meant. I have no alliance, I am neither human nor animal, and I hunt anyone or anything – for the benefit of those who pay the highest price."

"So now you will kill me? Or deliver me to the Vizier?"

"Yes, I may have to do either, but first I have a surprise for you. If you like my surprise, I will not have to hurt you. I would greatly prefer that because killing humans is so very messy."

"Messy? This is your only objection to killing?"

"Yes, Wicca. My only objection. Of course, it's also boring, unless I am hungry. You see, I am so powerful that no human weapon can prevail against me, so when I kill any of you I don't even have the fun of a good fight. Now, get into this tent. Someone is waiting for you." Having no choice, she obeyed.

Donna gaped. At the furthest part of the large, elegant tent, on a throne-like chair, sat Aunt Yolanda. She wore an improbable outfit consisting of a long leather coat decorated with gold thread, and a pith helmet, as if about to join a safari.

Sobbing, Donna ran toward her aunt, and threw herself into her arms. "Why are you crying, Donna?" Asked Aunt Yolanda calmly.

"Because I found you! Because I was afraid you were . . ." she could not bring herself to finish her sentence or stop crying. Gilbert, on the other hand, remained calm. He leapt off Donna's hair and sat on the ground, surveying the scene and ignoring Aunt Yolanda as if she were a total stranger.

"Oh, I'm quite all right," said Aunt Yolanda

casually. "I'm visiting with the Vizier."

"Visiting? I thought you were kidnapped. We all thought –"

"Who thought? These stupid camel and donkey? The aging queen and her incompetent prime-minister?"

Donna stared at her aunt. Strange, she thought. How did Aunt Yolanda know about the animals? And why was she so cold, so unfeeling? Moreover, Aunt Yolanda never insulted anyone, human or animal, never spoke of anyone with such contempt, and always treated everyone as worthwhile.

"So let me tell you about this place," continued Aunt Yolanda. "It's marvelous. The Vizier is truly a great wizard, and he intends to do wonderful things for Great River."

"Like starving the inhabitants and stealing the water?" said Donna. Why didn't Gilbert greet his favorite person, she wondered. And why didn't Aunt Yolanda even try to approach him?

"Oh, the inhabitants," said Aunt Yolanda carelessly. "They are not important. He will settle his own people on Great River, since there are untold riches to be collected there. We will be extremely wealthy, Donna."

"I am not interested in being wealthy. I never thought money mattered any to you, either. And what about my Wicca studies?" How come Aunt Yolanda didn't ask her about her travels, and if she felt well, and if she was hungry . . .

"Don't worry about that, child. You'll have the best training any Witch could ever hope for. We'll start you at the Wizards' School island, and from there – who can tell? We'll make you extremely powerful. Now give me the Cinnabar box, I must put it in a safe place."

"It belongs to the queen, really. What are you going to do with it?" asked Donna hesitantly. She was extremely suspicious now, but still, this was Aunt Yolanda!"

"I'd much rather you didn't argue and ask silly questions. Just give me the Cinnabar box, and I'll handle all the necessary arrangements," said Aunt Yolanda sternly.

That did it. Aunt Yolanda never objected to questions, she simply answered them, fully and concisely, whenever one wanted to know something.

"No," said Donna resolutely. "You are not Aunt Yolanda."

"Whatever in the world do you mean, Donna?"

"You are someone in disguise. Maybe that is why you are wearing this insane outfit. Illusion, probably, and you don't know what Aunt Yolanda normally wears."

"Nonsense. This is the way people dress here, so I wear it too, out of courtesy."

"The clothes don't really matter. Whatever Aunt Yolanda wears, she would never talk the way you did about the queen or the prime minister, or my animal friends. If you were Aunt Yolanda, wouldn't Gilbert jump on your lap? And how do you know about the flying animals, anyway?"

"Crystal ball," said Aunt Yolanda curtly. She seemed angry, her green eyes flashing. But she controlled her temper. "Now, are you going to give me the box?"

"No," said Donna, retreating. "No, I won't."

Something was happening to Aunt Yolanda's face. It was shifting, changing, as if made of computer images. Donna retreated further. Her aunt's robes, her hair, all became misty, gray and swirling. She turned into a whirlwind, swift and purple, and took herself out of the window. The elegant tent began to move, rumble and shake. Donna turned, grabbed Gilbert, and ran out as fast as she could. When she stood at a safer distance, she looked back. The entire oasis, tents, palm trees, water hole, animals – all shifted, turned, swirled like a desert mirage. In a few minutes not a trace remained of the camp. Instead, a collection of dilapidated wooden shacks stood around a filthy, tiny water hole and some miserable vegetation.

"Gilbert, I am beginning to wonder if it won't be better to join a rock group after all," said Donna. "I don't recognize magic when it's right in my face. I can't believe I didn't see the place was a mirage! And yet, why don't they just seize and kill me and take the Cinnabar box? Why do they only trick, and threaten, and play stupid games?"

Gilbert whined. He seemed to be just as fed-up with magic as she was. However, she spoke too soon.

"There is no escape, Wicca," said the hissing voice of the Peryton behind her. "Did you really think I will go away? I am so sorry that you disliked my little surprise. I thought the Vizier put up a beautiful illusion, but I suppose neither of us took human emotions into consideration, so we didn't realize you will see this was not your aunt. Didn't she look accurate, though?"

"Very," said Donna cautiously. "I almost believed it." She tried to prolong the conversation, but would he fall for it?

"Well," said Peryton, "we must be off. I have to take you to the Vizier as soon –"

But before he could finish his sentence, an avalanche of flying carpets swooped down on him. There were so many soldiers, flying carpets and flying animals, that the sun seemed to be eclipsed. Peryton fought. The soldiers threw giant nets around him. They could not kill him, but the nets, perhaps helped by magic, seemed to hold him prisoner. As soon as the strong horns slashed one net, another ensnared him. Donna crouched on the ground, holding Gilbert tightly against the pocket where she kept the Cinnabar Box and protecting him with her arms. She hid her face in his soft fur and waited until Peryton's shrieks and the soldiers cries were quieter. Then she looked up and saw Jaafar, in a soldier's outfit, jumping off one of the carpets and landing next to her.

"I am sorry, Jaafar," she whispered. "I should have never doubted you, but when he said you were the Vizier . . . and Taliesin warned me against the humans . . ."

Jaafar smiled. "Well, it all ended well. Very intelligent of you to leave this little note to Roxanne about going away with Peryton. I guess you trusted her because she was an animal?"

"Yes, and I figured she would know if you were the Evil Vizier or not. So I took a chance and left that note in the bathroom under her balalaika when I was dressing, and Peryton didn't even suspect."

"Very, very wise, little Wicca. Roxanne came straight to me, of course. Haroun-al-Rashid will use enchantment on Peryton and send him to another reality, hopefully forever. And the soldiers are releasing all the prisoners," said Jaafar kindly. "Let's go and see if your friends are there."

The shacks held many human and animal prisoners, all in pitiful condition. Chained to the walls and kept under magical formulas, they seemed sick and half starved. In one of the shacks Camellia and Bartholomew sat huddled together, reduced to almost skin and bone. Donna ran and hugged them both silently. Camellia sobbed and wrapped her wings around Donna, and Bartholomew muzzled her wet cheek and leaned his thin face on her shoulder. None of them could speak.

———————

The heavy wooden door burst open, and the prime minister ran into the queen's room with the unseemly haste that he usually succumbed to at moments of strong emotion. "Your Majesty!" he cried. "The agents and the little Wicca are back in Great River! I saw them flying in my crystal!"

The queen sat by the window with her head leaning heavily on her thin hands. Slowly she raised her eyes to her old friend. "They are back?" She whispered. "Are you sure? I have given up all hope, my friend. I am worn out . . ."

The prime minister strode purposefully to the crystal ball and removed the black cloth. He adjusted the buttons on the golden box and put the ball squarely on the table before the queen. An image shimmered and coalesced. There could be no mistake – Donna, sitting on the back of Camellia, Bartholomew by their side, the two animals flying vigorously against the gray, stormy sky, covered with clouds that never rained.

Outside, the hot, dry wind blew as usual, driving the dust against the heavy glass of the window pane. The queen stood and gazed, wordlessly, at two half-starved flying animals and one young girl, the three of them supplying the only thread of hope left for a dying world.

An uneventful flight that took forever, Donna felt, but by now she was so used to it she never even felt sick. Idly she wondered how the animals found any guideposts – the desert never changed.

"We are near the palace," said Camellia, as if she read her thoughts. "Look, here are some refugees." A small band of people, wearing gray and black tattered robes and shouldering small bundles of belongings, marched toward something that looked like a mountain. As they drew nearer, though, Donna realized her mistake.

The mountain-like structure was an enormous building, constructed from sand-colored, rough stones. It loomed so high that the clouds hid part of the roof. Around it stood ramshackle, rickety little gray huts, dry as bones, and black tents. A few withered trees and thorny desert bushes sprouted around the little village. For all its size, the palace still looked like an island in the ever encroaching waves of yellow-gray sand.

"These are the shanty towns we told you about," said Bartholomew, "the ones created for people whose water sank to the ground. Poor devils."

"At least they are alive," said Donna practically.

"Exactly – and now perhaps they will be saved," said Camellia joyfully. "Well, Bartholomew, we are finally home. Landing time!"

They landed precisely, beautifully, just in front of the enormous wooden gate of the palace. At the same moment, the gate creaked, slowly opened, and out came the queen and the prime minister.

"Welcome," said the queen softly. "Welcome, my dear friends. How I missed you." She put her arms around the necks of the two animals and stood quietly for a few minutes with her head bowed as if giving thanks for their safe return. The prime minister patted the animals on their backs, weeping openly and rubbing his eyes.

Then the queen raised her head to look at Donna. Donna gazed at the huge, black eyes, full of sadness, love, and understanding that encompassed all that there was in the world. They reminded her of Shape-Changer's eyes. It's the Wicca soul, a thought suddenly crossed her mind. The thought felt almost alien, as if it belonged to someone older than herself, perhaps her own Wicca soul.

"Welcome, my child," said the queen. "You are brave and resourceful, and I don't have the words to thank you for all you have done."

Too overwhelmed to talk, Donna took the Cinnabar box out of her pocket and handed it to the queen. Before the queen could take it, though, an enormous shadow suddenly fell on the ground and a sound of thunder crushed Donna with its violence. Mist, cloud, and shadow mixed to surround her, swirling like a purple whirlpool and isolating her from her companions.

"Well, Wicca, we meet again," rumbled the cloud. "What a pleasant reunion."

Donna could not answer, her throat too dry for speech and her mouth feeling as if it frozen.

"Hand me the Cinnabar box, Wicca," said the cloud.

Donna didn't move.

"Wicca, I have no time for the likes of you. If you don't obey, I will destroy Senior Witch Yolanda, plain and simple."

The terror that flashed through her was so intense she stopped feeling. She froze into a statue of ice in the eye of this living storm. Something, though, tugged at her consciousness, strong enough to restore her capacity of speaking.

"Then why don't you kill me, Vizier?" she asked in a hoarse voice. "You had many opportunities. Why are you wasting your time talking to me now?"

An incredible rumble shook the cloud and the earth under her trembled. She stood her ground.

"Why don't you just take the Cinnabar box, Vizier? Is there a reason you can't do it?" She could not believe she had uttered these words, actually challenging this frightening being.

Purple lightning shot through the cloud and through the sky above it. The blue mouth was twisted in rage and the yellow green eyes blazed. She winced and stepped back a step or two, expecting the final blow. Nothing happened.

"I don't think you can take the box, Vizier," said Donna with icy calm. "Something is stopping you. I will never, ever, give you the Cinnabar box. I am Wicca and I have my Code –"

Lightning hit the ground. A long fissure appeared in the earth, only a few steps away from Donna. She fell, half fainting, as the cloud lifted itself and disappeared into the sky in a purple tornado.

When she opened her eyes the queen, Camellia, Bartholomew, and the prime minister were hovering over her, trying to revive her with the little water they had. "I am all right," she said. "Why didn't he kill me?"

"Because it's not the Vizier in person," said the queen. "The image in the cloud is his disguise, his illusion, and in a way, his messenger. It takes a tremendous amount of power to keep it going, and right now he has to juggle many other illusions. Keeping the water hidden from an entire planet takes an untold amount of energy. The cloud could take the Cinnabar box to the Vizier, but it was not strong enough to make you release it unless you gave way to your fear."

"Please take the Cinnabar box, Your majesty," said Donna wearily. "I am not sure I can handle much more of that."

The queen took it gently, looking at it with reverence. "Yes, you are right. We will waste no time and go directly to the water source. All the people who live around here can take shelter in the castle. When the river is released, it will be some time until it finds its proper bed, and floods may occur."

"Can my lemur wait here?" said Donna. "He is tired, perhaps hungry."

"Of course," said the queen, gently stroking Gilbert's head. The animal licked her hand. "We will call someone from the palace to take special care of him."

The prime minister climbed with some difficulty on Bartholomew's back, and the queen and Donna mounted Camellia. As they flew away, Donna saw the long line of the thin, tired people carrying their bundles to the palace. They flew a short distance toward a range of mountains.

The mountain, sheer, dark, and covered with jutting rocks, loomed over them, hiding half the gray sky. "Now," said the queen. She took the Cinnabar box from her pocket and put her silver ring next to it. The carvings in both items fitted perfectly and the box suddenly burst open. Inside lay a tiny silver key.

The queen stepped forward, stuck the key into a small dark hole in the rock, and turned it carefully. In the total silence around them, Donna heard the creaking sound the key produced in the rock. For a few minutes nothing happened. Then the earth rumbled. Clouds of gray dust swirled around Donna, and as she coughed and choked, the rock walls started sinking into the ground slowly, relentlessly, seized by an irresistible force. She grabbed Camellia's furry neck, screaming with terror, but no one heard her through the horrible sounds of the earthquake. And suddenly everything stopped and the dust settled. The mountain disappeared, leaving nothing but a plain of yellow sand with some dark green, scrawny plants growing in it. But where was the water?

Donna looked at the queen, and shuddered when she saw the grief, the hopelessness, in the woman's eyes. "There is no water left in the land," whispered the queen. "The Vizier won. We are all lost, forever . . ."

"No!" Cried Donna, rage flooding her entire being. "I won't let this happen! And I must find Aunt Yolanda, too, she must be here somewhere, and she'll know what to do!"

"Child, look around you," said the queen, taking her hand gently, "He dried the source of water, and I don't have any magic left in me. There is nothing here, nothing but the dead desert. He must have hidden Senior Witch Yolanda in his island after all, or killed her. We are all going to die, anyway, and very soon. It's time to give up."

"Never!" Furiously tearing her hand away from the queen's, Donna ran into the desert. She ran until she could no longer breathe, the pain in her chest choking her in the searing heat. Almost fainting, she fell down, sobbing and scratching the hard, sandy ground with her mud-caked nails.

Her hand landed on a something smooth and round, warm to the touch. She looked at it through her tears and saw a golden, orange, perfectly rounded and translucent stone, like a miniature sun. It pulsated gently in the glaring light.

Donna's heart lost a beat. She had never seen such a stone, except, perhaps . . ."You will earn it or you will find it," her aunt said about the Wicca stone. Or both, Donna hoped. She touched it again, and it felt warmer. Aunt Yolanda's Wicca stone told her when Donna needed help. Perhaps this stone could tell her if Aunt Yolanda was alive. Feverishly, she dug the stone out of the ground and dusted it with her dirty T-shirt. Trembling with anticipation, she put it in the silver locket. It fitted perfectly and started pulsating faster. Slowly it turned darker, deeper orange. Donna stared at it, hypnotized, until a small movement caught her attention.

A tiny fountain of crystal-clear water flowed out of the hole in the ground that the Wicca stone left when Donna dislodged it. The water bubbled gently and streamed across the yellow sand. More and more water gushed out of the ground, pushing the sand out of its way. With amazing speed, the water rushed forward, no longer clear and gentle, but pink and gray, with swirling foam on powerful waves. The sky turned angry yellowish gray, as if an impossible storm was approaching. Donna turned and ran, trying to get away from the furious water, but it was too late. The rushing current seized and carried her in its path. Tumbling and turning, she did her best to swim and keep afloat. The river carried her toward the palace, through one of the deserted shanty towns.

The river hurled itself into the wooden village, destroying the rickety, decaying gray houses in its path. Donna managed to grab the crumbling boards of one of the porches that somehow remained standing and held tightly as the river continued its destructive way through the deserted village.

She held on, gasping and coughing water, when something swooped out of the sky. Camellia, wet and disheveled, landed on the porch, flapping her great wings. "Climb, quickly," she cried over the sound of rushing water. "We must find Aunt Yolanda!" Donna shouted, climbing on the camel's back. "I found my Wicca stone, Camellia! In the desert, it waited for me to come, I know that. I would have never found it if I had given up and stayed with the queen! Never! And the stone tells me she is alive, and not too far, so it will lead us to her!"

They flew above the rushing water. The stone turned light again, so Donna knew they were heading in the wrong direction. Following the darkening and lightening of the stone, they went through the agonizing search in every house left in the way of the river. But Aunt Yolanda was nowhere in this village. The darkening stone led them further back toward the palace.

Purple lighting illuminated the sky, momentarily blinding Camellia, and an opaque cloud, as thick as marshmallow, stopped their advance. "Look, Camellia, it's the Vizier's face in the cloud, but it's shifting, it's not so clear."

"He is constructing something solid out of the cloud to stop the river, I think," said Camellia. "It looks as if he is trying to build a dam."

On a rock under them, a man was standing, wailing and shrieking. He obviously used Sound Magic which needed so much power that he could no longer maintain the illusion of the horrible face in the cloud.

"But Camellia, it can't be done. No magic can fight the river. Let's try to stop the Vizier, he will kill himself."

"Serves him right!" said Camellia curtly. "Do you know how many lives he took in his greed and cruelty?"

"But he is the only one who knows where my aunt is –"

Camellia dived. "Vizier," screamed Donna. "Stop fighting the river – you can't. It will kill you. Come with us, surrender to the queen –"

The man looked up. Insane fury lighted his pale gray eyes, and he directed his wail at their direction. Camellia swayed under the attack.

"Don't, you miserable idiot!" shouted the camel, for once forgetting her manners. "We are trying to save you!"

The cloud dam shifted. The Vizier brought his attention back to it to strengthen it, and it stood firmly, for a moment blocking the river. And then the rushing water, pink and gray and immensely powerful, broke though it and washed the Vizier away.

"We must go back to the palace," said Camellia sadly. "The Vizier is dead. Perhaps Bartholomew will find your aunt, he has been searching other villages."

The queen waited for them with the Prime Minister. Gilbert balanced on her arm, and as soon as he saw Donna he leapt and wrapped his little paws around her neck.

"There is one more task for you to do, my child," said the queen. "We cannot regain our magic with sufficient speed. You have more strength, so you must be the one to name the Great River. Naming it will allow us to direct and control it. Otherwise, the power it unleashes may destroy too much."

"Later. I must find Aunt Yolanda first," said Donna. "She is here, I can see it in the stone."

"There is no time, Donna."

"I can't concentrate on magic when I am so worried, Your Majesty."

"You must. Concentrate. You must name the river," said the queen patiently. "Until our powers return, you are the only one who can do that."

"But look at the stone –"

"Stop arguing, child! The good of the people comes first. We will continue to look for your aunt, but you must name the river. You must concentrate."

Donna's mind was blank. She could not think about the river, other than it was about to destroy Aunt Yolanda, helplessly imprisoned with no magical powers to release her. She was also distracted by the lemur, who clung desperately to her arm, his ringed tail wrapped tightly around her neck. He stared at the rushing water with his great golden eyes and sniffed loudly.

"Please, Donna," said the queen sternly. "If you control the river you may save your aunt anyway. Let your mind find a name for the great river. Call the name loudly and tell the river to stop. That's all. It's easy – "

The lemur strained his little body, his eyes intent on one of the shacks, and suddenly leapt into the rushing water. Donna tried to catch his tail, but in vain. The lemur disappeared into the waves. "Gilbert," Donna screamed with all her might. "Gilbert, stop!"

A strange hush fell over the river. The water stopped rushing. The waves stood in midair. For a few seconds nothing happened, and then the waves rearranged themselves, and moving like marching soldiers, started contracting and organizing the direction of the water. Donna could see the lemur now, swimming steadily.

"Your Majesty," said the Prime Minister hesitantly, "I think Donna has just named the Great River after her pet lemur."

"I didn't mean to," said Donna apprehensively. I am so sorry – I just tried to stop Gilbert –"

"But why not?" said the queen, laughing. "Life is life. A small lemur is as important as a great river. And the mission is accomplished! The river is named, and restrained. The Gilbert River, now and forever."

"But it's still rushing madly through the village," said Donna. "It's breaking all the houses."

The queen smiled at Donna with indescribable happiness. "Don't you see?" she said gently. "It is good. The river is cleaning all the unhappy remains of our long years of suffering. Now that you have controlled it by the Naming Ritual, it will soon find its proper river bed and settle down to be a good, life-giving waterway. It will restore our prosperous world to us. I will build new houses for my people, clean, beautiful houses, and we will have fields and forests again, and flowers, too. I have not seen a flower for so many years, Donna. I think I am going to plant a rose garden."

But Donna wasn't really listening. At a distance, she saw someone swimming. Straining her eyes, she suddenly rushed forward, jumped into the water, and swam furiously. In any alien world or strange reality, she knew only one person who could behave so calmly under such circumstances. Only Aunt Yolanda would look so dignified with a fat lemur balancing on the top of her head, holding tightly to her floating auburn hair.

———————

Sitting quietly in a cool room, with a lemur wrapped around her neck and the river whispering outside, felt good. Donna dosed off, occasionally looking at the construction work outside. The inhabitants were so happy, she thought. What a pleasure to have been involved in returning their river, though their thanks embarrassed her. It was good to see Jessamine and her grandmother, too. They will never have to be so poor, ever again.

"My powers are returning," said Aunt Yolanda, sipping her coffee. "The vizier's death broke all the illusions. I can't tell you, Your Majesty, how strange it felt to be locked in this shack, unable to exercise Wicca powers to release myself. So when Gilbert unlocked the shack's door with his clever little paws – the joy of seeing him –"

"I can imagine," said the queen. "And I feel my powers returning, too, but of course it will take longer after being deprived of them for centuries."

"You managed to turn river water into this

incredible coffee already, Your Majesty. You are recovering very fast," said the prime minister. "How did you conjure these cakes?"

The queen laughed. "Well, all will slowly return to normal. Can you smell the moisture in the air? And what are your plans, Senior Witch Yolanda?"

"First, a vacation," said Aunt Yolanda. "Donna and I will spend a couple of weeks at the zoo. I spoke to Vainamoinen on the crystal yesterday, and he is coming to visit me there. Poor thing, he was so frustrated by being forbidden to destroy the Vizier. It would have given him such pleasure. Vainamoinen said he will bring Taliesin, since Donna promised him St. John's Wort medicine to cure his depression. We have plenty of that at the zoo. Then, perhaps, a visit with Shape-Changer. I want to start planning with him some way to save his race, and I have an idea of a special sanctuary attached to my zoo. Donna will help us with the selection and study of plants his people need, of course – her first assignment. Then, we will go back home and seriously start studying Wicca. I believe Donna has great talents."

"More important, she has courage and knows how to keep her wits about her," said the queen. "I will never forget the moment she cut Camellia's bonds with the broken lens from her glasses, and her note to Roxanne, the toad! Outstanding."

"True Wicca resourcefulness," said Aunt Yolanda with satisfaction.

"I knew you would say that, Senior Witch Yolanda. What about her parents?"

"They will not object to her staying with me, Your Majesty. I will give her a good education and much care. They know that."

Donna was suddenly wide awake.

"But does Donna want to devote her life to this dangerous work, Senior Witch Yolanda?"

"Nothing will keep me away from it, Your Majesty," said Donna. "It's much more fun than my original plan of being a rock star, and unless you sing like my friend Taliesin, a career in music is very difficult to get into in my world."

"In any world, I imagine," said the queen sympathetically. "My prime minister had some thoughts of going into show business, four hundred years ago or so, before I convinced him that getting into government was so much easier than -"

The prime minister cleared his throat. "It was a long time ago . . . no need to bring it up . . ."

"I believe you wanted to be a dancer, didn't you, my friend?"

Donna looked at the rotund figure of the prime minister and almost giggled.

"Shall we invite Jessamine to come with us on our vacation at the zoo, Donna?" said Aunt Yolanda quickly.

———————

To find that special place at the zoo, they walked a long stretch of a dirt road, glaring and overwhelmingly hot under the direct rays of the sun. Donna and Jessamine dragged themselves, kicking the dust, carrying the soggy brown lunch bags and bottles full of lukewarm water. Going on this trip without water was unthinkable; the dangerous climate had to be treated with utmost respect, even by semi-trained Witches.

They reached the ancient wall, built with the pink stones of the region. Little slivers of mica made the stones gleam under the sun, changing colors as the sun changed its position. At that hour the wall was dusty rose, almost the same color as the road. For some reason the huge stones felt cool, rough and comforting. A few enormous, unfamiliar lizards slept peacefully, balancing on the edge.

The wall had a narrow opening with no gate. Anyone could walk in and gasp, every time, at the sight of thousands of acacia trees, totally covered with yellow flowers. The acacia park was so large it could almost be called a forest. It stood on low hills, gently sloping toward the blue-green sea, a giant aquamarine gem without a single wave or a bit of foam to disturb its calm surface.

It felt unbelievably cool under the green shade of the acacia trees, as the breeze from the sea drifted into the park. With every gust of wind the golden dust from the acacia flowers fell like fairy rain on the girls' heads and clothes.

They walked toward the sea. The rocks on the white, damp beach had a sheer covering of glass formed naturally millions of years ago. Each broke a small piece for a keepsake. In this place no one had to think of conservation; everything existed in abundance. The glass mirrored the color of the sea, a little lighter, perhaps, and shone in the sun. Another aquamarine.gem, a tiny one which they could take home and keep forever.

They sat down to eat their lunch on a deep, thick carpet of emerald-green wild grass. Even wilted sandwiches and tepid water tasted delicious there. The golden light filtered in delicate patterns through the acacia canopy, its branches so thick it hid the sky. In every clearing, though, the grass gave way to enormous patches of cherry-red poppies and white daisies, like giant oriental carpets spread here and there in an enchanted palace. They ate quietly, listening to the birds and the hum of thousands of bees. The honey they made from the acacia flowers had a strong, wild flavor.

A small herd of dodo birds came up from the beach, and the girls fed them and stroked their smooth feathers. Two tiny, sleek creatures peeked at them with soft brown eyes from behind a tree. Donna recognized the eohippus, or four-toed horse, from a book about evolution. The creatures looked like living toys.

"You must promise to visit me again soon," said Donna.

"Of course. I have the coordinates, it's easy, and we are lucky that the realities coincide," said Jessamine. "We can hop back and forth after doing homework."

"Or cheat and do our homework together," said Donna. She groaned. "Double homework. Regular school *and* Witchcraft."

"It's not too bad," said Jessamine. "You'll get used to it."

"At least I won't have time to visit the country club . . . and I will never, ever go to summer camp!"

"What in the world are these?" said

Jessamine. "Your reality sure sounds strange."

"You don't want to know," said Donna. "Even Wizards' School Island is fun compared to a country club and a snooty girls' camp."

"Well, you will be busy for other reasons," said Jessamine, grinning.

"What do you mean?"

"I mean you will invite somebody else to visit as well . . ." said Jessamine slyly.

"Oh, you stop that!" Said Donna, laughing. "Really, Taliesin and I are just friends."

"Yes, right. That's why you never speak of anything else. Is he really as handsome as people say?"

"He is awesome," said Donna sadly. "Much too handsome for someone fat and ugly like me. But anyway, we are just friends, and he needs the medicine."

"You have lost weight in this adventure already," said Jessamine. "And I think you are lovely, and I am sure he thinks so too, and that he appreciates the St. John's Wort."

"Yes, Vainamoinen checked the medicine and told Aunt Yolanda that he liked the ingredients very much. He is really impressed, and now he wonders if it is ethical to use it in his reality, since it was invented in his future! I hope Aunt Yolanda will convince him to bend the rules a little. Eventually, I think Taliesin will be cured and wouldn't even have to take it anymore. And then he can start writing what he calls the Songs of Joy. Well, he is coming here tomorrow, so you will help me fix my hair a bit, won't you? It's a little longer already, I think.

Jessamine, you just have to hear Taliesin sing . . . and will you stop laughing!"

Donna found it hard to separate from the acacia park, even though Aunt Yolanda promised they would come back often to the zoo. To comfort herself, she thought that since she expected to specialize in Plant Wicca, she would come here to study the possibilities of these magnificent trees. Before leaving, the girls picked some flowers from the lower branches and put them in their hair. The acacia flowers looked like bunches of fuzzy, soft, yellow grapes, and smelled like a mixture of roses, honey, and warm, drying grass. A strong, insistent fragrance, not subtle at all, demanding attention, and even a little disturbing at times. It followed them out of the park, calling them back. For Donna, it will forever be the scent of summer.